5.95
6/73

D0482558

STETTLER MUNICIPAL
LIBRARY

Search for the

CRESCENT MOON

Illustrated by Bea Holmes

Eth Clifford

Search for the
CRESCENT MOON

STETTLER MUNICIPAL
LIBRARY

Houghton Mifflin Company Boston 1973

Also by
ETH CLIFFORD

The Year of the Three-Legged Deer

COPYRIGHT © 1973 BY ETHEL CLIFFORD ROSENBERG
ALL RIGHTS RESERVED. NO PART OF THIS WORK MAY BE
REPRODUCED OR TRANSMITTED IN ANY FORM BY ANY MEANS,
ELECTRONIC OR MECHANICAL, INCLUDING PHOTOCOPYING AND
RECORDING, OR BY ANY INFORMATION STORAGE OR RETRIEVAL SYSTEM,
WITHOUT PERMISSION IN WRITING FROM THE PUBLISHER.
LIBRARY OF CONGRESS CATALOG CARD NUMBER 72-13582
ISBN 0-395-16035-9
PRINTED IN THE UNITED STATES OF AMERICA.
First Printing w

In memory of my mother,
who carried pride like a banner

Author's Note

In 1778 a FIVE-YEAR-OLD CHILD named Frances Slocum was kidnapped by Delaware Indians and was presumed to be lost forever. Almost sixty years later, an Indian woman, feeling that she was near death, spoke to a white trader and revealed to him that she was white, that her family name had been Slocum, and that she had come originally from Pennsylvania. The trader got in touch with the Slocum family. Two brothers and a sister journeyed to Indiana and met the long-lost sister in the Bears Hotel in Peru, Indiana.

Following the reunion of the Slocum family, the brothers and sister tried to persuade Frances Slocum to return home with them, but she refused. Instead, a nephew and his family subsequently moved to Indiana to be near their aunt.

Frances Slocum died on March 9, 1847, and was buried beside her Indian husband and two of their sons. Today in Indiana there is a state forest in the Miami and Wabash counties that bears her name.

That is history.

On May 23, 1848, a man named John Dillon delivered an address to the Indiana Historical Society which said, in part:

> In the northern part of the state of Indiana on the 28th of November, 1840, the chiefs and the head men of the Miami nation were holding a council with two commissioners of the government of the United States. The council ground was at the forks of the river Wabash. A treaty . . . was laid before the red men. The first article . . . was in these words: "The Miami tribe of Indians do hereby cede to the United States all that tract of land on the south side of the Wabash River not heretofore ceded, and commonly known as the 'residue of the Big Reserve' — being all of their remaining lands in Indiana" . . . Thus the last remnant of the National Domain of the Miamis passed from them forever.

The Miami nation had been a powerful one in its time, its domain extending in Ohio west of the Scioto River, over all of Indiana, the southern part of Michigan, and that part of Illinois which lay southeast of the Fox River and the Illinois River.

In the early days of Indiana, when is was still part

of a vast wilderness known as the Northwest Territory, the Miami had their first contact with French Catholic missionaries, French fur traders and *couriers du bois*, "wood runners." The missionaries fought for control of Indian souls; the more practical traders and *couriers du bois* settled for furs and Indian women, showing little prejudice in their relationships with the Miami. Intermarriage was common, and there were many Indian children who claimed a French heritage through their fathers.

When the Miami eventually ceded their lands to the government of the United States, certain areas were set aside for Indians of mixed blood. Among these people was Chief François Godfroy, whose French ancestor fled from France to escape the French Revolution. Another person who received a large grant of land was Frances Slocum, who was white, but whose Indian husband had owned extensive acreage outside of Peru.

That is history.

Although this book was suggested by the Frances Slocum story, *Search for the Crescent Moon* is not history. Many of incidents in this book did occur; some of the characters did exist. But incidents and characters have all been utilized primarily to tell a story — not as it happened, but only as it grew in the author's mind. *Search for the Crescent Moon* was never intended to re-create an exact historical account of Indiana in 1840 but rather to explore and savor the American character of that era. Broad humor, rough justice, daring, adaptability and mobility were the clear stamp of the early nineteenth-century Hoosier.

Although historical inaccuracies occur — Chief Godfroy's home, for example, was not at Deaf Man's Village on the Mississinewa but on the Wabash River; the itinerant painter John Banvard never was aboard the *Republican* and his panorama was that of the Mississippi rather than the Wabash; the Peru Blues' "Chipanue" war took place in 1836; etc. — for the most part, this book has endeavored to be faithful to the era.

My grateful thanks go once again to Hubert Hawkins, Secretary of the Indiana Historical Society and head of the Indiana Historical Bureau, for his invaluable help in supplying and granting me permission to use source materials and for reading the manuscript to guard against glaring historical inaccuracies or inconsistencies.

Eth Clifford
Indianapolis
1972

Search for the

CRESCENT MOON

★ Prologue ★

1778

Mrs. Bright came to the doorway and looked out. In the yard she could see her son Nathan busily sharpening a knife. A neighbor's son, fourteen-year-old John Amis, marched at the head of some invisible army, his slight body encased in a soldier's jacket, shouting commands in a high shrill voice. Mrs. Bright sighed. The war with England still raged, a necessary war, but Quakers were people of peace. She sighed again as John turned smartly, saluted a nonexistent officer, and headed away from the yard. His antics brought her oldest son to mind — impatient Isaac, who, knowing his father would never consent, had run off to join the fray.

Mrs. Bright shielded her eyes against the cool but bright sunshine which made this November day glitter. They had been happy here, in this fertile valley that skirted the Susquehanna River — the Indian names, she thought, her mind skittering off from her fears for Isaac, were beautiful, as this valley was beautiful, as the river running clear and fresh through the land was beautiful. She had not wanted to leave Rhode Island to travel this long distance through forests to Pennsylvania, but when they had made their home here at last, she had been content. They lived in peace. Others had suffered from the hands of warring Indians, but not the Brights. The Indians had shown a curious respect for "the men of the black hats," as they called them.

A sudden movement obliquely to her left caught her attention.

"Joshua," she cried.

A small boy limped into view. Still painful, Mrs. Bright took note, the leg that had been broken and was taking so long to heal.

"Where is Sarah?" she scolded. Joshua and Sarah were twins; where one went, inevitably the other went as well. Then she saw Sarah's flaming red hair just at the corner of the house. Sarah's brilliant chestnut-brown eyes were spilling over with laughter.

"I hid," she shouted gleefully, "and Joshua couldn't find me. Could thee, Joshua?"

"Thee is too clever for me," Joshua said good-naturedly.

"Run inside, clever one," Mrs. Bright called to Sarah. "It is time to set the table." She smiled as Sarah rushed past her, shouting impatiently to Joshua,

2

"Thee must come and help too. Hurry, Joshua," and then, mindful of her brother's injury, racing back to take him by the hand, wishing to be with him yet straining to move as quickly as the spirits bubbling within her.

There was time yet before the men came in from the field to eat, Mrs. Bright thought, and once again her mind turned to Isaac. Seventeen, and a soldier, swept up by the fervor of the times, gone to protect this land from the British and from the Indians who fought with them. Arms and Indians! Most of the neighbors had fled to the sanctuary of the fort nearby, fearful of so lethal a combination. But not her husband Jonathan Bright. The Indians had never harmed them, why would they do so now?

"Unless thee wishes it, Margaret," Jonathan Bright had said. "If thee wishes to go to the fort, then I will take thee and the children."

"And thee will stay?" Margaret had laughed at her husband. "Who will see to thee if not me?" she chided him. "I have no fear of the Indians. They have been our friends since William Penn's time. They know we are people of peace."

And so the decision had been made. The Brights remained on their land, and their neighbors, the Amis family, had elected to do likewise. Day after day Jonathan Bright worked the farm, together with Margaret Bright's father, Isaac Tripp.

Mrs. Bright narrowed her eyes against the sun and looked toward the fields. She could not see her husband or father but she knew they were there. How saddened Jonathan had been last month when news had come to him that their son Isaac had taken up arms. The tranquillity of their home had been shattered. Jonathan could not believe that his eldest son could go against everything he had been brought up to cherish, a way of life that had brought the Quakers so far from their roots in England.

As Mrs. Bright stood in the doorway brooding, her husband and father, working in the fields, suddenly ceased their labor. A sound had alerted them. Jonathan removed his hat, mopped his brow, and then clapped his hat back on his head again. He felt a certain unease, a feeling so new to him, so inexplicable, that he decided to go back to the house sooner than usual.

"We have done enough this morning," he said amiably, then stiffened with surprise. The Indians who approached seemed to have materialized from the earth itself. He noted that they carried guns — a war party; yet he was sufficiently calm to call a greeting. "Ollawachica is welcome," he said, recognizing one of the men, the man whose name meant "loud voice." The Indians surrounded the two men, but left the talking to Ollawachica, who immediately cried accusingly, "Quakers are men of peace, and yet the son of the man with the broad-rimmed hat kills his Indian brothers."

"He is young and does not think," Jonathan began, but before he could continue, Ollawachica struck him down. "Let him think now when he comes home and finds we are brothers no more."

"Margaret, warn Margaret," Jonathan whispered to

4

the older man before Ollawachica's blows silenced him but Isaac Tripp went down, dead before he hit the ground, when another Indian struck him from behind. The war party did not stop to scalp the men but headed silently for the house. Ollawachica had sworn revenge as soon as he had heard that young Isaac was carrying arms against Indians and British. Nothing would appease him now but death to the entire Bright family.

Margaret was in the kitchen supervising Joshua and Sarah. She was scolding Sarah for unseemly conduct; Sarah was prancing beside the long table, mocking John Amis, marching, shouting orders, saluting. She was a perfect mimic; Margaret had to suppress a smile even as she reprimanded Sarah. "All this time in the kitchen," Margaret said, shaking her head, "and not one dish on the table nor . . ." A child's terrified scream transfixed her in mid-sentence. Margaret's voice faltered; her hand flew to her throat. "Nathan!" she cried, racing to the doorway, the twins at her heels, and was stricken dumb at the sight of John Amis savagely struck down — his soldier's coat, so infuriating to the six vengeful Delawares, already deeply stained with his young blood — and her son Nathan . . . Margaret stretched her hand helplessly before her, as if this one small gesture could stop the carnage. Then, turning swiftly, she whispered in a voice that commanded instant obedience. "Sarah, thee is so clever at hiding, go and hide at once, and take Joshua with thee."

Sarah looked up at her mother's grim face, took

Joshua by the hand and urged him quickly to a small enclosure under the stairway. It was dark in the closet, and close, but the door was ill-fitting, and some air seeped in through the bottom of the door where it swung free of the floor. Margaret, meanwhile, fled from the house through a side door and hid in a thicket where she positioned herself so that she could keep a watchful eye on the house.

Sarah and Joshua huddled together, their hearts thudding, and listened to the sound of footsteps pounding through the rooms, up the steps and down again, into the kitchen and out. The children froze as the footsteps, which had receded, grew louder and then stopped. Ollawachica had grown curious about this doorway under the stairs; he flung the door open, and he shouted triumphantly when he saw the boy and girl standing together hand in hand. He reached out and seized Joshua; Sarah reacted quickly, aiming a kick at Ollawachica's leg and shouting, "Thee leave Joshua be."

Ollawachica grinned. "A brave heart to go with the hair that burns like the sun," he said. He handed Joshua to the Delaware who had come to join him, and took Sarah casually from the closet and tossed her over his shoulder.

Margaret, from her vantage point in the thicket, saw the men emerge from the house with the twins. She sprang like a tiger from her hiding place and confronted them. "Ollawachica, I beg thee, not the children. See," she pointed to Joshua's leg, "the break

is not yet fully mended. He cannot walk far. He will only hinder thee . . ."

Ollawachica gestured to the brave who held Joshua. The Delaware released the boy, shoving him forcefully to the ground where Joshua lay, momentarily stunned.

"Hair that flames I shall keep," Ollawachica said flatly.

"I beg thee," Margaret pleaded. "She is but five years of age. Ollawachica, I implore thee, in the name of God . . ."

But Ollawachica was already running, the other braves at his side, while Sarah from over Ollawachica's shoulder cried, "Mama! Mama!"

Margaret pursued them like one possessed, with Joshua tumbling painfully in her wake, on his bruised leg, but at last she fell back sobbing, her hands clapped against her ears as if to shut out the last shrill cry, "Mama! Mama!"

In one day, Margaret Bright had lost father, husband, son and daughter. She went through the days that followed in silent shock, moving out of her numbness only if Joshua moved from her side for any reason. Friends had come; they had made the plain coffins and carried them to the Meeting House. The small congregation sat in silence, as if it were a meeting for worship. Any member of the congregation would have been free to rise and speak, again as if at meeting, but no one felt moved to do so. So they sat, and then, as quietly, left the Meeting House and carried the coffins to the graveyard. There were no services — Friends could speak or not, as the spirit moved them. But again they were silent, and when the earth covered the coffins, they filed out of the graveyard and walked quietly back, some to their homes, others to the nearby fort where they still sought refuge from reprisals.

Only Margaret and Joshua remained behind, Margaret white-faced and brooding, Joshua pale with the heavy burden of the days just past. Suddenly Margaret fell to her knees and seized Joshua, pulling him close, frightening him with the intensity of her grip.

"Thee shall find our Sarah," she said fiercely. "Though it takes thee till thee is old, thee shall find our Sarah. Thee must promise me thee will never stop searching for her."

"I promise," Joshua answered. Then he added practically, "But if it takes me until I am old, then Sarah will be old too. How shall I know her when I see her again?"

Margaret clutched Joshua's right hand and turned it palm upward. She pressed her finger upon the fleshy part of his palm.

"The birthmark, Joshua. Sarah has it, too, in the palm of her hand." Joshua stared down at his hand and the white semilunar scar, then up again into Margaret's luminous eyes.

"Thee must search for the crescent mark on her hand, Joshua," she commanded him urgently. "Remember it always. Thee must search for the crescent moon."

CHAPTER

★ 1 ★

1840

Although the path they traveled was a sucking sea of mud, both the fifteen-year-old boy and the man on horseback were enchanted with the brilliance of this May day. It had rained the night before, but now the spring sunlight washed the foliage a gold-flecked green; the air, clean and fresh, still carried remembrance of the crispness of winter past; birds, chirping, calling, darting swiftly, still went single-mindedly about the business of nesting or feeding their young. The path itself was lined on either side by trees that reached upward almost one hundred feet in the air, standing like a protecting wall through which the travelers progressed.

About noon the older man suggested to the boy that they dismount and rest, and having done so, stretched himself wearily out upon the grass, thankful for a change of position. The boy wandered off a little way, curious, stopping to marvel at the play of shadow and light; unconsciously, his fingers drew shapes in the air, while in his mind's eye he filled them in, here the deep shades, there a whisper of light. Catching himself, he glanced about guiltily, as if he had been found in some reprehensible act, and turned to come back along the path. Turning, he caught sight of what appeared to be an abandoned campfire, yet baking nicely above the banked fire was a well-done side of deer. He approached cautiously, called out once or twice, then went closer. Peering down at the ground, his wide mouth split into a grin, and he ran speedily back to where the older man was dozing.

"Grandfather. Grandfather," he shouted, shaking the other awake. "Thee must come and see. Someone has prepared dinner for us."

Protesting, the other rose grumpily to his feet. "Thee has a vivid imagination, Tobias," he complained. "How many times must thee be told thee must learn to curb it. Dinner for us indeed," he grumbled as he followed Tobias slowly along the path. Tobias ran ahead, looking back like a frisking pup to ensure its master's following, and came to an abrupt stop near the campsite he had seen moments before.

"Look there, Grandfather. Does thee see what someone has written?"

Joshua Bright peered down at the ground, then moved closer so he could read the words that had

11

been scrawled in the ground: *Eat and welcome, whoever you might be.* Some thoughtful hunter had obviously killed and dressed a deer, consumed what he had needed, and then had carefully salted and baked one side of the deer before breaking camp. He had, prior to departure, then turned the other side of the deer toward the banked fire. By the time Joshua and his grandson had reached the campsite, the venison had been done to a turn.

"Like manna from heaven," Joshua Bright murmured in awe.

"As thee says," Tobias agreed sunnily, running his tongue over his lips in anticipation, "the Lord has provided."

"Thee must not be frivolous," Joshua reprimanded the boy sharply. Tobias sighed. There were so many restrictions and none, he thought for a moment rebelliously, more restrictive than the injunction that he could not draw or paint. It was nought but a sensual gratification, the brethren said, and as such was opposed to those spiritual feelings which should constitute the only perfect enjoyment of a Christian. Games of chance forbidden; music forbidden, instrumental music being neither a source of moral improvement nor of solid comfort to the mind, and vocal music capable of being most detrimental to morals. Dancing forbidden; the reading of fiction forbidden; the theater and playacting forbidden. Tobias knew the principles of the Society of Friends well, and did not chafe against any, except that he could not draw on paper those images that burned in his mind.

Tobias sighed again. "I am not frivolous, Grandfather," he said plaintively, "only hungry."

"Then thee must eat," Joshua said gently, and admitted, when they were satisfied at last, that never had he tasted a better meal.

Tobias tore his hat from his head, leaned back against a huge walnut tree, and breathed in the air deeply. His hair caught fire from the sunlight which filtered down through the leaves; his chestnut-brown eyes, unusually light and brilliant, reflecting the red of his hair, were now half-closed and dreamy. Joshua, watching his grandson smilingly, closed his own eyes as well, only for a moment or so it seemed, to wake with a start when Tobias nudged him, and said reprovingly, "Grandfather, thee will sleep the day away. Thee said fifteen or twenty miles would be a good day's journey, and we surely have not come more than ten so far."

Joshua rose at once, a slender, spare man with a lean bony face, a wide mouth and the same lively eyes as his grandson, although lacking their brilliance.

Tobias clapped his hat back on his head, remounted his horse and waited patiently for his grandfather to ride beside him.

They came presently to a creek, whose angry swirling waters, swollen by the rain, Joshua regarded dubiously.

"We must cross," he told Tobias, but he stayed irresolute, somewhat dismayed at the prospect of urging his horse to the water's edge. It was then that Tobias heard voices upstream.

"Perhaps there is a ferry of some kind further on, Grandfather," he said. "I can hear people talking."

The two pushed on, following the banks of the creek, and were soon rewarded by the sight of two sturdy young men cutting down a tall hackberry tree, long dead but apparently recently stripped of its bark by enterprising woodcocks in their eager search for worms. The tree fell with a crash that resounded in the woods. A wagon was stationed beneath the shade of a huge maple, and beside it, a woman and two girls were busily engaged in guarding a flock of sheep. An older man, tall rawboned and good-humored, with a booming voice and an even heartier laugh, greeted the newcomers to the scene.

"Welcome to Brown's Wonder Creek," he roared jovially. "We mean to ford it here, and we can use the extra hands, if you be willing."

Joshua and Tobias dismounted, secured their horses and approached the younger men, ready to do whatever they were bid.

"What is it thee plan to do?" Tobias asked curiously as the men swiftly cut the fallen tree into sections some twelve to fourteen feet.

The others glanced at one another, somewhat taken aback by Tobias' speech, but then the youngest son answered courteously, "We're going to build a raft so we can take the wagon and supplies across."

"The wagon?" Tobias echoed, turning to stare at it and then at the logs nearby. It could not be done, obviously, since the wagon was large and heavily laden and the logs skimpy; the proposed raft seemed scarcely large enough to hold the men, but Tobias was too polite to express his doubts aloud.

Tobias helped place the logs side by side, and then watched as the two brothers skillfully laid poles across them and secured them by boring through the poles and into the logs with an auger. In addition the father, with Joshua's assistance, made a canoe, little more than a trough, yet large enough for three men. The canoe apparently would need to be steadied by one or both brothers lying flat on its bottom to act as ballast.

Joshua mopped the perspiration from his brow, for he was unaccustomed to such backbreaking labor, but the three men worked on almost tirelessly while the father chatted amiably. They were the Hunters, he said, recently of Nicholas County in Kentucky. Born and bred in North Carolina he was, wed in Pennsylvania. Not many Quakers hereabouts in Indiana, but he had seen them aplenty in Pennsylvania — this he inserted in the flow of talk as he glanced obliquely at the clothes Joshua and Tobias wore. "My wife liked Pennsylvania fine, easier on her I don't miss my guess, but people became thicker than game, if you take my meaning," he roared amiably. And so they had gone to Kentucky, stayed there a while, and now they were going to settle the other side of Brown's Wonder Creek, for how long he was not prepared to say, because you might say he was a rolling stone. But the boys wouldn't move on. They took after their mother, sort of clung to what they knew; but he couldn't say as how he blamed them as there were eighty good acres of farmland waiting if they put their backs to it.

15

At length Joshua broke in to ask, "How does thee propose to take the wagon across the creek?"

"How? Easy as pie. We'll just unload it and take it apart. You there, Willis, Webb. Let's see to the wagon now. You, too, young feller," he shouted to Tobias.

Willis swung himself up into the wagon and began to hand out everything within it into the willing hands of his family and Joshua and Tobias Bright. The work went quickly and soon everything in the wagon was lying neatly some little distance away. Then the wagon was pulled apart before Tobias' astonished eyes.

"Will they be able to put it together again?" Tobias whispered in an aside to his grandfather. Mr. Hunter, passing by, laughed and pounded Tobias on the back. "Don't you fret none, son," he roared jovially. "We've done it afore, and we'll do it again."

Now everything the raft could hold safely was piled aboard, and Willis and Webb swiftly attached about two or three hundred feet of bedcords to the raft. Then the two young men leaped on the raft, each with a firm grip on a ten-foot pole. Mr. Hunter took to the canoe; then, having persuaded Tobias and Joshua to lie flat, choking with laughter at using Quakers as ballast, he handed them the rope ends. He now directed the canoe cautiously along the shore, while Willis and Webb poled the raft behind them. Tobias, turning his head to glance at his grandfather, was almost convulsed with laughter himself. Never had he seen his grandfather in so comical a position nor so utterly astonished at finding himself so!

The canoe and raft made repeated trips back and forth across the creek, carrying the burdens precariously to the other side, where everything at long last waited to be reassembled.

Finally it was only a matter of bringing the sheep across the creek, but here the problem suddenly became more troublesome than anything that had gone before. Time and again the sheep, bleating and complaining, were forced into the water. Willis and Webb went into the creek, calling, cajoling, shouting, but the sheep stubbornly insisted upon returning to the same side. They would not cross the creek!

"Mr. Hunter," Tobias said, approaching the frustrated, bellowing man rather shyly. The man brushed him aside impatiently, leaping after one of the sheep who was trying desperately to scramble up the bank of the creek, and shoving it irascibly back into the water. "Mr. Hunter," Tobias tried again when Hunter passed him once more.

"Tarnation, son," Hunter cried in exasperation. "What is it?"

"I know how thee can get the sheep across."

"Does thee now?" Hunter mocked. "And how might that be?"

"If thee will put two of the sheep in the small craft with me . . ."

"The craft? Which craft? Do you mean the canoe?"

Tobias nodded. "The others will follow," he said.

"Well." Hunter considered the suggestion. "They sure aren't getting across now. Willis! Webb! Get

17

two of these consarned sheep into the canoe."

Willis and Webb seized two sheep, thrust them unceremoniously into the canoe, laid them flat on the bottom, and then poled the small craft to the far side of the creek where the terrified animals sought refuge on land. Scurrying free, they instantly set up a plaintive bleating. Across the water the other animals echoed their cry. The Hunters once again forced the flock into the creek; this time they made no attempt to swim back but headed for the two sheep on the far bank.

Tobias and his grandfather forded the creek on horseback, where Joshua eyed with some misgiving the activity of the Hunters. They were now reassembling the wagon with great vigor and speed. The Hunters urged Joshua to stay on a spell, but he was weary of the whole business and bade them farewell, explaining that he and his grandson had still a far way to go. Furthermore, night would be coming on soon and they would have to find shelter before dark.

"You'd best stay on with us," Mr. Hunter urged, sending a knowledgeable glance upward. "It's fixin' to rain soon."

But Joshua was adamant. Mr. Hunter, he discovered to his chagrin later, was right. The rain did come. It pelted down mercilessly, a punishing, driving downpour that soaked Joshua and Tobias within minutes. The horses whinnied and struggled against the reins with each clap of thunder that reverberated through the woods. Joshua could barely keep his head erect. He should have listened to Hunter; by now, no doubt, they had built a shelter of some kind. Any shelter would have been welcome, would have offered some respite from the rain which was assaulting them with such driving fury.

"A cabin," Tobias shouted suddenly, his voice high over the gusting wind. "Does thee see it, Grandfather, just ahead in that clearing?"

Joshua peered from under the brim of his dripping hat. To his left some little distance away a small single cabin sat lonely in a clearing, and next to it a somewhat smaller building, a shed, probably a stable. With one accord, Joshua and Tobias directed their horses toward the cabin.

When they arrived and pounded at the door, it swung open hospitably, and they were bidden to enter.

"The boy can see to the horses," the owner of the cabin said, and directed Tobias to the stable where, the man vowed, Tobias would find fodder in the loft. Tobias led the animals to the smaller building, which like the cabin was built of logs but unlike it not chinked with clay. It was anything but waterproof, as Tobias soon discovered, but he sheltered the horses as best he could, taking the saddles from their backs and the bits from their mouths. He looked for something with which he could rub down the horses, but the shed was bare of essentials. His lips compressed, he glanced up at the loft where the fodder was stored, thinking that the animals would have to shiver but at least they would be fed. He mounted the steps cautiously, for they had been thrown together in haphazard fashion from open logs. When he saw the fodder, Tobias' face flushed with anger. The fodder consisted of cornstalks so long exposed to the weather they had become blackened and thick with mold. Still, the horses needed to be fed; reluctantly, Tobias brought the cornstalks down and was surprised when the animals fell upon them with great appetite. Once again Tobias looked around for something with which to curry the animals. At last he seized some of the fodder and made do with rubbing the horses down as best he could with the stalks.

The rain had ceased by the time Tobias had attended to these chores. When he walked back to the cabin, he found his grandfather sitting before the fire, chatting amiably with the family. Tobias studied the cabin with interest. On their trip thus far, he and his grandfather had stopped at taverns overnight; this was the first time they had taken refuge in someone's home. There was but one room to the cabin, but it was fairly large and boasted a good-sized fireplace. Two large beds occupied two sides of the room, and a cradle, roughly hewn and shaped from a log, was in one corner near the beds, and in it lay a baby, staring at its own clenched fist with gurgling wonder. A long narrow trestle table was pushed up against a third wall, and the rest of the furniture consisted only of some splint-bottomed chairs. An effort had been made to brighten the walls with whitewash. The only decoration on the walls were wooden pegs, from which the family's clothing hung in full view.

The room was swarming with children of all sizes, from the baby in the cradle and the toddler who regarded them in wide-eyed amazement, fist crammed in his mouth, up to the oldest sister, a girl about Tobias' age. The mother was so careworn that she seemed to Tobias' young eyes to be older than his grandfather. Mr. Isaac Brooks, the owner of the cabin, was a slim, spare man with a tremendous forehead, sun-bleached hair, and pale eyes that were in strange contrast to his browned face. He was a man of few words, so few in fact that when he spoke, no matter how trivially, what he said seemed important.

The family had been about to sit down to the evening meal of fried pork and johnnycake — cornmeal mixed with salt and water until it formed a stiff dough, then baked on the hot stones of the fireplace. Places were set for the visitors, and everyone fell to at once, silently. Tobias bolted his food, with particular pleasure in the johnnycake, which he had not tasted before, but he surreptitiously pushed aside the concoction Mrs. Brooks referred to as tea, a hot drink she had made from sycamore bark.

As soon as the meal was over, Mr. Brooks asked abruptly, "Where be ye heading?"

"To a place called Deaf Man's Village," Joshua replied. "Near Peru," he added, when Mr. Brooks stared at him blankly.

"Deaf Man's Village," Mr. Brooks repeated suspiciously. "Sounds like one of them Indian names." Joshua acknowledged that it was indeed an Indian name. "Then how come you to hear of it?" Mr. Brooks was accusing. "We've been in Indiana goin' on for fifteen years and I ain't never heerd of it afore."

"Well, Peru is a mite far from us, Pa," Mrs. Brooks said timidly from her seat at the fireplace, where she sat carding wool, "and it could be Mr. Bright has business there we know aught of."

Joshua nodded. Mrs. Brooks had hit the nail on the head; he had business there. Two years ago a man had written a letter, addressing it to the postmaster of the town in which Joshua lived. The letter spoke of a white woman, newly released by the Indians, who remembered that she had come originally from Pennsylvania and was seeking to establish some contact with her family, if any member of it still lived. The postmaster had read it and cast it aside, thinking the matter of little importance after all these years. Subsequently he had died. His successor, in clearing the office, had accidentally come upon the letter, read it and mentioned it casually to one of the Quaker brethren, who in turn had rushed to Joshua Bright's home with the news. And so Joshua, taking his young grandson along as his companion on this arduous trip, had once again begun a journey. He admitted that he had made many such over the long years, and until now, had always found nothing but bitter disappointment at trail's end.

"This woman you're looking for," Mrs. Brooks questioned sympathetically, "someone real close to you?"

"A sister, a twin sister, kidnapped in 1778."

"In 1778?" Brooks repeated incredulously. "And you think she's still alive?"

God moved in mysterious ways, Joshua told his listeners quietly, and if it was His will . . .

Mr. Brooks opined he was as God-fearing as the next, but if ever he'd heard of a man wasting his time . . .

Joshua thanked his host for his hospitality and said that he and his grandson would take their leave now. They still had a great distance to cover, and each day's ride was bringing them nearer the end of his quest, of this he was certain.

They weren't planning to leave now? Mrs. Brooks murmured, aghast. Why dark would be coming on in another couple of hours. They would be right honored if their guests would share their cabin overnight. There were trundle beds, and the boy could sleep on the floor if need be. Then, in the morning, when they were rested and refreshed, they could continue . . . But Joshua was adamant. A glance around the crowded cabin convinced him that even if he and Tobias were to sleep that night beneath some welcoming tree they would be more comfortable and more at ease than in this room that overflowed with people.

Joshua offered to pay for their meal, but Mr. Brooks would not hear of it. They were welcome, and he wished Mr. Bright luck in a lugubrious voice. Tobias fetched their horses from the shed, and he and his grandfather, happy to see the sun had come out again, rode off after a last farewell.

Joshua and Tobias were pleased to be by themselves

once again; they cantered peacefully along the path, an Indian trail that led them to the banks of the Wabash. The water, high along the banks, was so clear that Tobias could see the fish swimming beneath the surface. The river glinted in the dying afternoon sun; the branches of the overhanging trees were reflected in the water below, creating patterns that absorbed Tobias. In his mind he translated the gentle scene to paper; here he would place the deepest shadows, there he would delineate the graceful arch of the branches. The desire to paint this quiet beauty was like an intolerable ache within him. Bemused, he scarcely heard the sound that startled his horse, a small chirping sound, like that of a locust perhaps. Behind him, Joshua pulled his horse up short. He had spotted the large snake moving slowly across the path.

"Tobias," Joshua warned, and saw that Tobias, too, had become aware of the snake now coiling, its rattles sounding, its eyes venomous. The boy looked about helplessly; the path was too narrow for him to swing wide of the snake; neither he nor his grandfather wished to turn back. It was, apparently, an almost insoluble dilemma. As Tobias glanced back at his grandfather, his eye was attracted by the sight of a forked branch which lay broken and leaning against a nearby tree. The branch was some eleven feet in length, and easily an inch or two thick. Tobias seized the branch and before his grandfather realized his intent, Tobias had advanced upon the snake and

struck at it with his improvised weapon. Again and again he struck, but his aim was not true. The snake uncoiled and slithered away, leaving behind a shaken boy and an even more agitated grandfather.

"We had best seek shelter for the night," Joshua said. "We should be sighting a tavern soon. I was told in Indianapolis that there were taverns hereabout."

Tobias pressed his horse forward with good will. It had been a long day and he thought longingly of a soft bed and a downy coverlet.

Twilight came almost imperceptibly. One moment the sun lingered in a spectacular blaze of color on the western horizon, the next moment the quiet blue of evening encompassed them. And then a curious light appeared where but seconds ago the sun had dropped from sight. It was as if the sun had risen again.

"Fire!" Joshua cried, and sent his horse galloping ahead. Tobias spurred his own animal. Just over the gentle rise in the land, they came upon a small cabin burning. Even as they approached, the walls collapsed. In a short time, nothing remained but smoldering ashes. A man and woman stood by helplessly, their faces pale with shock. They wheeled about sharply when they heard the horses' hooves, and the man raised his rifle and held it steady. When he saw the man and boy, he lowered it wearily.

Joshua and Tobias dismounted and asked how they could be of service. There was nothing anyone could do, the man said bitterly.

"Did Indians do this?" Tobias asked.

"Indians?" the woman scoffed. "Why the last time

Indians attacked a settlement was way back in 1815," she declared. They themselves had been living peaceably here since 1823. She wasn't denying that it had been hard. The first year they had planted corn, but the blackbirds had come, thousands of them, darkening the sky. "It was as if there was a bird for every ear of corn," the woman, who said her name was Mary Gain, remembered. They had been so discouraged they were going to pull up stakes and go elsewhere. And then the Indians had come. They had taught John Gain how to hunt and trap, and the next spring, they had come and helped plant a new crop of corn. The Gains had purchased a yoke of oxen and John had even begun to trade with the Indians, bringing them flour and blankets and other items, in exchange for furs. When her husband left her on his trading trips, the Indians watched over her, sending an old woman to keep her company the long lonely nights her husband was away.

One night the old Indian woman had become ill. Mrs. Gain had done everything in her power for the old woman, for whom she had great affection. She had not even gone to bed, but had sat in her rocking chair close to the fireplace so she could tend to the woman if need be during the night. Then, at two o'clock in the morning, Mrs. Gain went on, a catch in her voice, the old woman had risen, wrapped her blanket around her, come to Mrs. Gain. She had sat on the floor beside her, leaned her head against Mrs. Gain, and quietly died. Mrs. Gain had eased the old Indian to the floor, covered her gently, and had sat with the body until daylight crept in through the cracks in the cabin.

The old woman's grandson arrived to bring his grandmother back home. When Mrs. Gain met him at the door and told him the sad news, he said nothing but left at once. When he returned, a large group of sorrowing Indians came with him.

"They asked me to bake a cake in the ashes of the fireplace," she said, tears streaming unchecked down her face, "so they could bury it with her."

"The chief has always been our good friend," Mr. Gain added. "It was by his order that we were never disturbed. Whenever I left home on business, the chief sent someone to watch over my wife. Never have they shown us anything but friendliness."

"Then the fire was an accident?" Joshua inquired.

"No accident," John Gain said grimly. "Oh, there were savages here all right. But they weren't Indians. They're a gang of sneaking, murdering, cutthroats, and their leader is more vicious, more terrifying than any Indian you'll ever meet. Slade. That's his name. A white man."

"A devil," Mrs. Gain added bitterly. "John met him on one of his trips up north. He tried to take the flour John was bringing back, and John fought him off. He swore revenge." She looked at the dying fire. "He has had it, to be sure."

"What will thee do now?" Joshua asked sympathetically.

"Build again," John Gain said and reached for his wife's hand. "We cannot offer hospitality," he said

28

to Joshua. "But if you will ride along with us, but a mile from here there is a tavern where you can stay the night."

The tavern, when they reached it, was the most welcome sight Tobias had seen all day. It was quite large, two stories high, with a swinging sign that read *Entertainment for Man and Beast*. Their horses having been seen to by an obliging stable boy, Tobias stumbled up to bed after his grandfather. He thought that his eyes would close and he would be sound asleep even before his head rested on the pillow; but once in bed, he found that he was wide awake after all. To the gentle snores of his grandfather next to him in the bed, Tobias relived the day — the venison at the abandoned campsite, the encounter with the Hunters, the battle with the rattlesnake, the brief stay with the Brooks and then the burning cabin. All in all, a full day to be mulled over, and yet only one name seemed to be seared into his brain — Slade.

CHAPTER

★ 2 ★

TOBIAS GAZED WITH INTEREST at the river. He was standing at the foot of Main Street in the bustling little town of Lafayette. A ferry flat was moored on the eastern bank of the Wabash, the shining river whose curves they had followed for several days prior to their arrival at Lafayette; a skiff, a skillfully-constructed canoe, two pirogues and a keel boat were also moored there. Tobias' roving glance idly made note of several cabins scattered along the banks of the river, and then moved on to watch with interest the arrival of the steamboat which he and his grandfather would presently be boarding. Joshua had wished to continue the journey on horseback, but had easily been persuaded in favor of the river ride. His old bones, he admitted freely, could do with some respite from the jogging, and, in truth, he was somewhat excited at the thought of actually traveling via this unusual mode of transportation.

Suddenly an explosion ripped the air. It was followed by a stunned silence and then loud confusion. People scattered and ran for safety, then headed for the source of the uproar, Wylie's general store and post office. Tobias ran with the rest, coming into the store in time to see the proprietor himself, semi-conscious, lying among shards of broken crockery and a shivered door facing. Crockery on the shelves had broken as well, and other items had crashed down, the litter decorating the counter fore and aft. At length the dazed man staggered to his feet, inquiring of all within hearing, "Is Mouser safe?"

"*Mouser?*" an outraged voice in the gathered crowd shouted. "Here you almost blew us all to kingdom come, and you stand there fretting about a *cat?*"

"Well, he's a good cat," Wylie replied peevishly, peering around nearsightedly, but the good cat had very sensibly disappeared.

"What in tarnation happened this time?" another voice in the crowd called out.

"See that tree stump yonder?" Wylie pointed to the fragments of a huge stump that stood some little distance from the post office. "Well, I filled that with no more nor less than about a half pound of powder — Dupont's best," he added, aggrieved, "and then applied a match to it, a slow one. But I've got to say I might have made a little mistake . . ."

"Which being?" asked a jovial man who had helped pick up the bruised Wylie.

"Which being, Sam," Wylie twinkled back, "putting in that blasted peg to plug up the auger hole on the side facing me!"

Sam obliged with a hearty roar of laughter that almost knocked Wylie off his feet again.

"And while I was sneaking a look around the door to see what it was doing," Wylie continued with great good humor, "darned if the powder didn't catch fire, and there was that plug sailing through the air aiming right at me! I was never so scared in my life. I said to myself right then and there, Reuben R. Wylie, I said, you're a dead man. Next thing I knew, the plug shivered that door all to pieces, and I never saw nor heard nothing after that. You sure you ain't seen Mouser?" he asked anxiously.

"That cat has more sense than you," Sam replied, kicking the bits of crockery out of his way. "I think you better close up and go on back and lie down for a spell. You still look a mite worn."

Tobias left the store with the others, stopping to examine the shattered stump on his way back to the landing, then running to join his grandfather, who had begun to grow uneasy at Tobias' absence.

"Thee surely does not wish to miss the boat," Joshua reprimanded his grandson.

"Nor the trip along our beautiful Wabash," a voice said behind Joshua. "We are fellow passengers, sir," the voice went on. "Allow me to introduce myself." The voice, Joshua discovered upon turning, belonged to a man easily six feet tall, his posture straight as a gun barrel, his face massively square with the ruddy texture of the outdoorsman whose skin reddens but does not brown, and the look of a man with bulldog tenacity. "Major Nimrod Makepeace Loofburrow."

Tobias stared at the Major with frank wonder. The Major was dressed in uniform. The epaulettes on his shoulders were colorful, as was the scabbard which sheathed the sword that dangled at his side; but the uniform itself was distinctly shabby and appeared to have shrunk somewhat over the years, for there was space between the end of the trousers and the Major's shoes, as well as between his large broad hands and the cuffs of his jacket.

"This is a great moment," the Major confided. "We have the honor to be sailing on the *Republican,* the first steamer to go up the Wabash as far as Logansport."

"If we make it," someone said. "Now, Major, don't take offense. You know we're bound to hit a sandbar or two along the way." The newcomer offered his hand to Joshua. "Alpha Judson, of Peru, Indiana," he said.

"Alpha likes his little joke," Major Loofburrow muttered, obviously irked.

The contrast between the two men was remarkable. Judson, slight of build, fair-haired, gave the appearance of great candor and openness. Even standing still, he appeared quick and deft in his movements. Joshua and Tobias liked him at once; indeed, his charm and courtesy would have been most difficult to resist. Like the man himself, his humor was quick and ready.

33

"Does thee think we will really hit a sandbar in the river?" Tobias asked eagerly. The trip promised to be even more exciting than he dreamed.

"We'll soon find out, won't we?" Judson replied. The activity around the landing had increased. The townsfolk were flocking to the river's edge; there was much laughter, and shouts echoed back and forth from men on the river and those on shore. A holiday spirit pervaded the air. It was like a huge picnic to which everyone had been invited. Tobias and Joshua followed the others aboard.

The captain had promised that the *Republican* would leave Lafayette promptly. He was a man of his word, for at the appointed hour the steamer moved surely away from the landing to the sound of great cheering from the onlookers left behind.

It was a bright day. The river glittered in the sun, and Tobias, peering over the rail, could see far below the surface of the clear water. Stepping back quickly, meaning to call his grandfather's attention to the fish swimming below, Tobias backed smartly into a young woman who had just approached the rail. She made a small sound—*oof*—and sat down somewhat abruptly. Tobias turned scarlet with embarrassment; but before he could offer to help her to her feet, a man turned from his position at the rail and swung her easily back onto her feet.

"The West is a dangerous place, ma'am," he said gravely, "filled with Indians and young boys." Tobias observed the young woman with interest. Her honey-brown hair fell smooth and straight over her shoulders;

her eyes were hazel, but he could not determine whether they were green or blue or brown, for they seemed to change color with the light.

Rowanna Ashton smoothed and straightened her clothing. "I am prepared to deal with both," she answered soberly. Tobias, looking from one to the other, thought they seemed very much alike, the same serious voices, the same inward laughter that lurked behind the eyes.

"The river is so beautiful," Tobias said. "I was only going to tell Grandfather . . ." But, turning, he saw that his grandfather was engaged in conversation, albeit reluctantly, with Major Loofburrow.

"Yes, the river is beautiful," she agreed. "And its name is beautiful too."

"The Wabash?" Toby asked blankly.

Rowanna Ashton nodded. "Indian names have a special cadence, so unlike our English names." She lapsed into thoughtful silence. She had been enchanted when first she heard the name Deaf Man's Village. And now here she was, aboard the *Republican*, on her way to Deaf Man's Village to apply for a job as schoolteacher there. She was exhilarated; she was apprehensive. Her emotions, she admitted wryly to herself, were chaotic.

"May I join you at the rail?" Rowanna asked Tobias. Taking his consent for granted, she moved to stand beside him. The man, who said his name was Pierre Le Cateau, stationed himself on the other side of Tobias. Yes, he replied to Tobias' obvious curiosity, his ancestors had come from France. They had come to the New World, as they called it then, before there was a United States, when Canada had still been called New France, and Indiana had been a stretch of wilderness no white man had ever seen until Robert de La Salle had traveled down the Wabash with several white companions and the help of Indian guides. His great-grandfather, a young man of adventurous mind and a restless nature, had found his way from New France to the junction of the St. Mary and St. Joseph Rivers, where the Maumee River began, and had traded with the Indians at Kekionga. This great-grandfather, whose name had also been Pierre Le Cateau, had traveled up and down the Wabash, as far south as the Louisiana territory, as did other French fur traders. Then he had returned up the Wabash, carrying his furs across the portages, and had made his way down the Maumee as far as Lake Erie.

"How does thee know all that?" Tobias inquired, impressed. He could visualize the keen-eyed young man of that long gone time, strong, mocking danger, traversing the still waters through the forests that claimed the land, a free spirit who followed his instincts; Tobias could easily imagine the man standing beside him in his great-grandfather's place.

"Letters and diaries that Great-grandfather left behind. His spelling was bad," Pierre said gravely, "but he knew how to tell a story."

"And your great-grandmother?" Rowanna Ashton asked. "Surely it was a long way for a young French girl to travel?"

"Great-grandmother was an Indian. Her name was Topiah, which means 'frost on the leaves.'"

"What a beautiful name," Rowanna said, repeating the words softly.

"What else did he write about in his diaries?" Tobias asked with interest.

Pierre Le Cateau shrugged. "Many, many things. Like Robert de La Salle, Great-grandfather came from a noble family of France. Like De La Salle, he too grew bored with life at home and turned his eyes and hopes to a new land. But sometimes he was homesick, and then he wrote of the things he remembered in France with great longing. But mostly he put down the things he noted on his trading trips. Much about the Indians. Everything he ever saw or even heard about them. For example, Great-grandfather wrote" — Pierre closed his eyes and recited — "*This day I have seen a man of the Ottawas, his nose pierced with a ring, a tribal ceremony? This is not common among the Ottawas but I learned that far to the West there lives a Nation de Nez Percé . . .*"

"A Nation of Pierced Noses?" Rowanna interrupted with astonishment. "Surely not pierced noses!"

Pierre Le Cateau opened his eyes, made a small *tsk*-ing sound with his tongue, and continued, ". . . *because they pierce the nose, where they attach a little stone, much embellished, which falls to the middle of the mouth between the two lips. A whole nation so adorned! Would they not be a wondrous sight!*"

"How can thee remember so much?" Tobias was amazed. "When I am at my books, I can scarce remember one line."

"It is my only book," Pierre confessed, "and a companion to me on my own trading trips."

"Could I read it sometime?" Tobias asked eagerly.

Pierre Le Cateau shook his head. "It is written in French."

"I wish he had written it in English," Tobias sighed.

Le Cateau burst into laughter. "And so he would have, had he not been so foolish as to be born in France."

"Who was born in France?" a voice boomed behind Le Cateau.

Pierre wheeled around to see Major Loofburrow and Joshua Bright standing behind him.

"It is a long story, Major," Pierre said.

"Well there won't be time to hear it," the Major replied jovially. "While you and the young lady were speaking, we passed Cedar Bluffs and Davis' Ferry, and we'll soon see the Delphi landing. We'll be in Logansport before long."

"An excellent way to travel indeed," Joshua Bright said happily. If it had not been for the Major's constant stream of chatter, Joshua would have been quite relaxed these past hours.

The little steamer passed the Delphi landing, as the Major predicted, within a short time. Rowanna left the others standing at the rail and went below. She had not been gone long when the steamer suddenly jarred the passengers, some of whom lost their balance, as it ground into a sandbar and stuck fast. Rowanna came rushing up, frightened and pale, terrified that the boat was foundering and that all aboard would drown. She collided with Alpha Judson, who said reassuringly, "Just a sandbar, ma'am. The crew will have us going in no time."

As the passengers watched, the crew jumped into the water and began to strain and tug at the steamer in an effort to jog her free. But the *Republican* did not move. Captain Towe shouted commands; the crew shoved and pushed and lifted; still the steamer held fast. On deck Pierre Le Cateau grew impatient. He jumped into the water.

"Get some men on shore," he shouted, "and throw them a rope. They can pull as we push." At once several of the crew made for the banks, holding a large rope that extended clear to the shore.

Pierre and the other crew members began to push again. In a moment, they were joined by other passengers, among them the Major and Alpha Judson. Tobias begged his grandfather to let him leap into the river too, but Joshua would not hear of it.

"Thee is too young," Joshua said, "and not accustomed to such labor. Thee will get hurt." So Tobias stood on the deck with Rowanna, his lips compressed, and looked on with misery in his eyes.

Just when it seemed as if the *Republican* was permanently stranded, she suddenly moved and was free. A great cheer went up on board, while the men in the water grinned and congratulated each other on a job well done.

"One of the hazards of river travel, ma'am," Major Loofburrow commented to Rowanna when he was back on the steamer. "But we've seen the last of our problems now."

"What would you care to bet?" Judson asked cheerfully.

"I am not a betting man," the Major replied stiffly.

"Would you care to make a wager about the rest of our trip, Le Cateau? Mr. Bright?"

Le Cateau grinned, a slightly crooked front tooth lending his smile a rakish look, and said he had learned long ago not to bet against Judson. Mr. Bright said nothing. Tobias was surprised. He thought surely his grandfather would explain that the Society of Friends forbade the "custom of laying wagers upon any occasion whatever, or of reaping advantage from any doubtful event by a previous agreement upon a moneyed stake." Why Marcus Fell had been read out of meeting for buying and selling stocks, because games of chance, lotteries, and stock transactions were strictly forbidden.

It was just as well that no one took up Judson's wager, for the Wabash snared the little steamer relentlessly every few miles, and crew and passengers alike spent more time in the river than out, literally shoving the *Republican* up the river by brute strength. The sun moved with more alacrity across the cloudless sky than the boat did on the water. When the rays of the sun had deepened in the west, and the horizon turned scarlet, then faded into the deep purples of oncoming night, the *Republican* had almost reached

Tipton, where at last it stuck fast upon the bottom of the river and refused to be budged.

Joshua Bright, who suffered from occasional bouts of sciatica, decided to retire for the night, but somewhat reluctantly gave Tobias permission to stay up and look at the stars awhile. The night air had a sweetness that Tobias could almost taste; the universe stretched endlessly into the far reaches of space before his dreamy eyes. Rowanna, who had been walking back and forth on deck, stopped to talk to Tobias.

"I am so glad you're here," she said. "I have just met an old friend aboard, John Banvard, and he has promised all of us a great treat. He is going to show us a panorama. I think you will find it most interesting."

"A panorama?" Tobias was puzzled. "What is that?"

Rowanna laughed. "It's rather a fascinating idea, I think. John tells me the idea is not a new one, nor is it his. But knowing John, I am sure he has adapted it for his own purpose. Come along, Tobias. I think you'll find it more interesting if I don't stop to explain it."

Tobias followed Rowanna willingly into the lounge, where the passengers were seated, the hubbub of conversation and the expectant glances creating an atmosphere of excitement. If Tobias had ever been permitted to enter a theater, he would have recognized the bustle and stir that animated an anticipatory audience. Rowanna and Tobias found seats behind Pierre Le Cateau, who turned and smiled when they arrived.

41

A young man was fussing on the makeshift stage with two upright cylinders which apparently were to be operated with a crank. At last when all the adjustments had been attended to, he lifted his head and greeted his onlookers.

"Ladies and gentlemen," he said. "My name is John Banvard. You might call me an itinerant painter. What you are about to see, in a sense, is one huge painting, a panorama of the beautiful Wabash. I put my impressions on canvas in a series of scenes. I then attached them to these cylinders," he gestured toward them and then to the crank, "and as I turn this handle, the panorama will unfold before your eyes."

As Banvard stepped back, Tobias made a half-hearted attempt to leave his seat.

"Is something wrong? Are you feeling ill? It is rather close in here," Rowanna whispered.

"Grandfather would be very angry," Tobias agonized. "Painting is forbidden, and indulging the senses, purely for pleasure, is forbidden. But the truth is, I find it hard to leave."

"Then you must stay," Rowanna said firmly. "I shall make it clear to your grandfather that you wished to leave and I did not permit it. And that is certainly true, for you cannot miss this historic moment. John is an excellent painter. He has worked very hard and deserves our undivided attention. So please sit down, Tobias. We are disturbing the others."

Tobias sank down gratefully. He scarcely heard the lecture that went with the paintings, as scene after scene unfolded before him, all in all thirty-five scenes unrolling on more than ten thousand feet of canvas. It had been a stupendous task for the artist, requiring years of labor, yet it was over all too quickly for Tobias.

After the lecture, Rowanna introduced Tobias to the artist; Tobias, his mind full of dreams, could hardly keep his mind on what Banvard was saying. In a few moments, he excused himself politely and joined his grandfather in their sleeping quarters. Whatever the new day would bring could surely never equal what he had seen this night, he thought.

The next day the little steamer did battle again with the river, and once again was defeated. Everything conspired against the *Republican*. Two crew members were injured, and several passengers, having volunteered to tug the ropes on shore, tired of the whole business and decided on the spur of the moment to walk to the nearest cabin and purchase horses, and to continue their travels as the Lord meant them to do, not aboard some device fashioned by the devil.

"Fools to abandon their post," Major Loofburrow told Rowanna Ashton grimly. His manner indicated that if they were under his command, they would never have been allowed such unmilitary behavior. "She's moving now. If they had waited, they'd be seeing us arrive in Georgetown Rapids almost any minute."

Rowanna sighed. "How far is Georgetown Rapids from Logansport, Major?"

"About seven miles, Miss Ashton." Alpha Judson

seemed to have popped up from out of nowhere. "But ascending the rapids . . ." He shook his head. "I seriously doubt it."

"May I ask why you took this trip in the first place?" Major Loofburrow demanded with irritation. "You've done nothing but complain since you've come on board."

"I? Complain?" Judson denied it laughingly. "I'm a realist, Major, that's all. I've been in the water so often on this journey I think I'm growing fins. Am I right, young Tobias?" he asked, turning round and round. "Have I begun to grow fins?"

Tobias grinned. He liked Judson, who seemed to take matters so lightly, but who worked as hard as anyone else whenever the *Republican* was marooned on a sandbar.

"No, sir," Tobias said soberly. "Thee has no fins — yet," he added.

At Georgetown Rapids Judson was proved right. The steamer, as if it had determined that it was too frail to face the rapids, promptly clung to the bar. This time Joshua yielded to Tobias' pleading, and allowed him to join the crew and the passengers in the water, where he stood with the others, pushing and straining against the boat as the Wabash rose gently up to his chin.

"I think you would be better off on shore, helping with the ropes," Le Cateau said after Tobias' face had gone under the water several times.

"I think there is much in what thee says," Tobias

gasped. From deck the work had looked like fun, but standing in the water for two hours had lost its appeal. He turned to see how the men were faring on the banks, and clutched Le Cateau's arm. "Look," he whispered. "Indians!"

All along the banks, sitting and watching the antics of the white men and the boat that was supposed to move mysteriously under its own power along the river, were Indian men, women and children, utterly amazed, constantly amused.

"Potawatomi. And Miami," Pierre Le Cateau said.

"I've offered the Captain a one-hundred-dollar bonus as a premium, and the honor of being the first steamer to go as far as Logansport," Judson sighed on the other side of Le Cateau. He didn't even glance toward the Indians lining the shores on both sides of the Wabash. "But I don't think either he or the *Republican* will make it."

"Shall we abandon ship?" Le Cateau suggested. "Go ashore and find our way to Logansport?"

Major Loofburrow stiffly refused to join them. He knew where his duty lay, even if others didn't, and he made it clear that he would stay with the *Republican* until such time, be it even a week or more, that she sailed gloriously into the landing at Logansport. Going on board to rest, he expressed surprise that Joshua, who had struck him as a man of principle, also decided to join the others in finding another means of transportation. But when Rowanna Ashton announced her intention of leaving the *Republican*, the Major, surprisingly, was understanding and even gallant.

Tobias, walking past the Miami and Potawatomi, was somewhat fearful, for he had never been this close to Indians before, but the Indians ignored the group that passed and concentrated all their attention on the boat in the river, applauding and shouting when the *Republican* moved slightly and moaning when it slipped back onto the bar.

Judson, who proved to be very resourceful, commandeered a wagon and a farmer's son to drive it for the seven remaining miles to Logansport. They were jounced and jolted and jostled, but they were moving! In Logansport, Judson told them, they could buy horses — Miss Ashton could travel by coach, if she desired, he added considerately — and travel sensibly the rest of the way to Peru.

Joshua Bright and Tobias must be his guests while they were in Peru, he insisted. From what Joshua had told him on board the *Republican*, he had no doubt that Mr. Bright would find his sister quickly.

Tobias was delighted when his grandfather accepted. Looking up at Alpha Judson's open smiling face, listening to his quick, pleasant voice, Tobias was sure he would not meet anyone so good and friendly ever again.

CHAPTER

★ 3 ★

COME IN, AND WELCOME," Alpha Judson said warmly. "Please feel that this is your home for as long as you need it."

"Thee is very kind," Joshua replied.

Judson brushed his thanks aside. Perhaps some day, he said laughingly, he might wish Joshua to do as much for him. Were he to seek refuge in Joshua's home in Pennsylvania, would he be welcome? Whatever the circumstances? he added. At Joshua's look of surprise, he changed the subject abruptly. He walked to the fireplace, which dominated the room.

" 'Tis a most handsome fireplace," Joshua commented, impressed that it seemed almost possible for Judson to walk into the chimney from the generous sweep of the hearth.

Judson patted the chimney. "It was designed for me by an artist."

Tobias' attention was caught. A chimney designed by an artist? How strange! He had never heard anyone called a chimney artist before.

Judson chuckled at Tobias' expression. Not a chimney artist, but a chimney-witch. He held up his hand to fend off the next question trembling on Tobias' lips. Yes, he knew it was a peculiar phrase, but nonetheless the men who designed and built these special chimneys were known as chimney-witches. The idea rather pleased him, he confessed. It was a good cat-and-clay chimney — no, he said, catching a glimpse of Tobias' next question forming in his eyes, not because a cat might find it a welcome spot to curl up before the fire. The fuzz was taken from the cattail spikes and mixed right in with the clay, and why this specially prepared clay was superior he wasn't prepared to say. Chimney-witches, Judson went on, were expert at so framing the flue of the chimney that the smoke was properly drawn up and out and the heat projected into the room, instead of the reverse. And he had choked in enough cabins, he added, to appreciate having smoke rise in a flue rather than circulate in the room.

As Judson was speaking, a woman entered the room followed by a young girl. They were obviously mother and daughter, for while they did not look alike — the mother was fair, with pale hair of an indeterminate shade that might have been blonde or gray, and blue eyes that seemed to be washed clean of color, firm tight lips and an ample figure, while the daughter was small, dark, with vivid flashing eyes and a spirited manner — they both moved with such determination that one was almost an echo of the other.

"Come in, come in," Judson said amiably, although they were both not only in the room but half way across. "My housekeeper, Mrs. Dolly Bladen. And her daughter Catherine."

Mrs. Bladen acknowledged the introduction briskly, while Catherine studied Tobias frankly. Her eyes swept over him, absorbing his clothing, his speech, as he sprang to his feet and expressed his pleasure at meeting them, and even, or so Tobias swore later, whatever thoughts may have flitted through his mind at the moment.

"If the gentleman wishes to rest," Mrs. Bladen said, "the room is ready."

Joshua admitted that he would like to take advantage of this offer, for the long trip from Pennsylvania to Indiana had been more tiring than he had expected. At age sixty-seven, he added, one tended to need more comforts.

"If you like," Judson offered, turning to Tobias, "while your grandfather rests, I can show you the grounds."

Tobias was delighted. There was so much to see, he did not wish to sit idly by and wait for his grandfather to recover from his weariness.

"If thee doesn't mind, Grandfather?" he asked

politely. Joshua waved his hand in dismissal. "If I were fifteen," Joshua said sympathetically, "I should be riding off in all directions at once."

Joshua followed Mrs. Bladen up the steps to the upper story of the cabin. There were two bedrooms upstairs, one a fairly large pleasant room facing west with a good-sized window through which a breeze gently whipped the curtain in and out.

"Here, now, we can't have that," Mrs. Bladen said, and the curtain suddenly hung gently without moving, as if the tone of her voice had abashed the wind and shamed its playfulness. She closed the window firmly, then, having ascertained that she could do nothing further for Joshua, left. Joshua went to the window and opened it again. Looking out, he experienced a great sense of peace as his eyes drank in the tranquillity of the creek just beyond the gentle slope of the pasture. He felt heartened. He had taken so many journeys, had gone, over the years, on so many quests to find the crescent moon. Would he find Sarah now, the Sarah who still remained in his mind the impish, gleeful five-year-old who had said: *I hid and Joshua couldn't find me, could thee, Joshua?*

He had never been clever at finding Sarah when they were children. Would he be better at it now? Going to the bed, Joshua sank back upon it gratefully and within a matter of minutes was sound asleep.

Tobias meanwhile was riding beside Alpha Judson. Judson had explained that the main building, the house in which Tobias and his grandfather were guests, had been built by his father. It was a generous-sized, two-story cabin made of rough logs covered with clapboard. The puncheon floors inside were slabs of hard wood that had been split from oak blocks of the right length and then carefully smoothed on the upper side with an adze. The slabs were six feet long, three feet wide, and four inches thick, if Tobias was interested in such statistics, Judson added with a grin. The adze was a cutting tool made of iron. It was wide, had a sharp edge and a long wooden handle. Tools were not that crude any more, Judson said, but when his father had built the cabin, he had had nothing more to work with than the froe, a forerunner of the ax, with its wedge-shaped cutting edge at the end of a heavy wooden handle. And of course he had used a mallet, which was a hammer of sorts.

Tobias nodded politely. He was, in truth, very little interested in such details, but having lived all his life with his grandfather, had grown accustomed to the idea that older people had a tendency to reminisce at great length.

Judson directed their horses around the back of the cabin, pointing out a lean-to on the north side of the house. This was the kitchen, which had been built in the same fashion as the cabin, but because of the slope in the ground, was a full story lower than the main building.

The house itself stood on a small hill. From the rise on which they had paused momentarily, Tobias looked down the slope to the creek, the same creek his grandfather was studying from the bedroom window upstairs. Judson now urged his horse to the east. Tobias,

51

following, noted that the hill on this side ended in a shallow ravine. Across the ravine he could see the outbuildings, one a surprisingly large structure proving on closer inspection to be the Judson stable.

"I have never seen such a large stable," Tobias said with surprise.

"I am a horse trader," Judson said. "True, I have fifty acres cleared for farming, but that's only, I think, to be quite honest, because the land is here. I own it, and it is good rich soil. But my only love is horses."

"I didn't know anyone could own so much land," Tobias said frankly. "Grandfather is a farmer, and we have the house we live in and the land it sits on, but it is nowhere near so grand as all this."

Judson laughed. "It is grand, isn't it? I own more than six hundred acres, good land, well timbered, well watered, finely situated. I would not change places with any man."

"It's like a dream," Tobias agreed.

Judson looked at the boy beside him, and his eyes sparkled with mischief. "It was a dream. I mean it. Let me tell you how it began, Tobias." They dismounted, and Judson leaned his arms on the fence that enclosed the stable grounds. "My grandfather was English. His name was Andrew Forbes Judson. He had traveled to this country during the French and Indian War." Judson was amused at Tobias' blank look. "What, you don't know your history? England and France were mortal enemies, boy. They fought on land, they fought on sea, and, believe it or not, they extended their battles to this country. The French and the English fought here, and both sides got the Indians to help them. That was what brought my grandfather here. He was sent to enlist the Indians on the side of England. The Indians called my grandfather Warraghiaghy, meaning 'he who takes charge of affairs.' A good name, considering the kind of man he was. At any rate, Grandfather was a bit of a dandy, who brought along clothing more suited to fancy London society than the wilderness, but Grandfather was a man to get dressed for dinner if he was sitting down to bread and water."

Tobias could easily picture the English dandy. He was so clear in Tobias' mind that, had he had a sketchbook in hand, he could have drawn the man as if the living model stood before him. Judson went on speaking; Tobias, listening, saw the scene as if it were unfolding before his eyes.

One day Andrew Forbes Judson was regarding several of his suits critically when Keokuk bounded into the room. Andrew Judson had tried to explain what the word privacy meant, a concept which Keokuk had found delightful but meaningless as applied to himself, and finally had resigned himself to having Keokuk continue to appear and disappear at will. Keokuk was fascinated by the clothing Judson wore. He would come and finger every garment, sometimes as it lay upon a chair, other times as Judson was wearing it. The name Keokuk meant "watchful fox," and there were times when Judson believed that no fox ever watched its prey more assiduously than Keokuk stalked Judson.

As usual Keokuk picked up each garment, and as usual exclaimed over it. Then suddenly he turned to Judson and said broodingly: "Warraghiaghy, Keokuk had a good dream. Keokuk's dream was so good he had it one time, two times, three times."

Judson fluffed the lace on his cuffs critically. "And what did the Good Spirit show you in your dream?" Judson inquired indifferently.

"Warraghiaghy was in my dream." Judson stiffened; the dream could serve him well, or not, for whatever the dream foretold must come to pass. Keokuk was most superstitious about the power of dreams and could be ruthless in their fulfillment. "Warraghiaghy showed me his clothes, good, kind Warraghiaghy, and told Keokuk to choose whichever he wanted, and Keokuk chose this one," he ended triumphantly, pointing to Judson.

"But I have never worn this before," Judson gasped indignantly, then, seeing how swiftly Keokuk's expression changed, added blandly, "but if my brother dreamed his dream, he must have the suit." Whereupon Judson calmly stripped himself until he stood bare before the Indian, then found another set of garments to put on. Keokuk left in a swirl of ecstasy. No other member of the tribe would now compare to his sartorial splendor.

A week later Keokuk reappeared. Before Keokuk

could speak, Judson seized him by the hand and said urgently, "Brother, I have also had a dream, a strange but pleasant dream that has been bright and clear before my eyes, even when I am awake. Once, twice, three times I have had this dream."

A dream three times repeated was powerful magic. This Keokuk well knew.

"My dream showed me a bright morning. The sun was brilliant over the wide forests and the laughing waters. The big trees wore crowns of golden light; the birds made the woods ring with their songs. The air was fresh and sweet. The Great Spirit smiled his blessings on the earth. Then I heard a voice calling, 'Warraghiaghy! Warraghiaghy!' I looked and saw my brother Keokuk beckoning to me from yonder hilltop. I climbed to his side and Keokuk pointed to the wide woodland that began at the creek and ran to the river, eight arrow flights wide and sixteen arrow flights long. As he pointed, he turned his kind face to me and in a voice of music said, 'Warraghiaghy, take this land, my brother.'"

Keokuk was stunned. The tract of land that Andrew Forbes Judson described so coolly covered more than six hundred acres of fertile land, beautifully located.

He swallowed hard. "My brother dreamed this dream three times?"

"Three times," Andrew Judson said firmly.

And so the land had changed hands.

Tobias was silent. Alpha Judson observed him shrewdly. "You don't approve, my young friend?"

"It seems not honest to me, sir," he said frankly. "Does thee think it was?"

Judson shrugged his shoulders. "Keokuk was a scheming rascal. If he could have diddled my grand-father, he would have. Anyway," he said, yawning, "even though many of the tribes have been moved west, enough Indians still remain who are big land-owners. Why on the other side of the creek, Little Bear Woman owns almost eight hundred acres. And there are many like her still in these parts."

Then Judson smiled at Tobias engagingly and spoke about having to attend a meeting of the Peru Horse Thief Detective Association, a meeting he couldn't miss since he was the president. He said gravely that it was open to members only or he would invite Tobias to accompany him, something Tobias might surely enjoy since they had secret handclasps, and secret passwords which each man had to whisper before entering the room. With a last cheerful wave of his hand Judson rode off.

Tobias looked after Judson, remaining thoughtful long after the other was out of sight. He had been deeply disturbed by Judson's story. Retelling it later in the day to his grandfather, Tobias said, "His grand-father was no better than a common thief. He cheated the Indian. What's more, Grandfather," he went on, coming at last to the heart of his grievance, "thee should have seen his face when he told me the story. He thought his grandfather was clever to have gotten the land."

"We cannot hold Mr. Judson responsible for the actions of someone else, Tobias," he said reprovingly. "And surely thee must have misread his meaning. Mr. Judson has been a kind and considerate host. We must not be so quick to judge him or any man."

Tobias agreed reluctantly that perhaps he had been too quick in his judgment. However, when dinner was over, the evening spent, and everyone had gone to bed, Tobias felt too restless to sleep. He had been given the east bedroom, opposite the room in which his grandfather was staying. Tobias went and stood by the window, then he dressed quickly, left the house quietly and made his way slowly down to the creek.

Once there, on impulse he removed his shoes and waded across a small shallow rapids which swirled over three large flat rocks imbedded in the creek. He was off on what he intended to be no more than a brief reconnaissance of the land on the other side. The evening air was soft and balmy; the creek slipped its silvery way past the clusters of hawthorn and wild plum bushes which flamed at every gentle shimmer of moonlight. He walked on, and walking, dreamed; if ever he learned to paint, could he capture on canvas the enchantment of this solitary stroll, the garlands of wild flowers that scented the night, the colors, subdued in shadow, leaping to quiet brilliance when moonlight glanced down upon them briefly and then moved on, the night sounds of creatures never glimpsed, even the cadence of his footsteps as he moved aimlessly forward?

Suddenly, like an apparition, a fox ran past, so close Tobias could feel the animal brush by. It barked as it flew past, a cry of warning? of terror? Then even as Tobias froze where he stood, the fox reversed itself and came tearing back. The tranquillity of the woodland was shattered. The fox was gone, fleeing into the dense shadows of the grove just beyond Tobias' position, but behind him branches in the bushes crackled, and a series of sounds reached Tobias that frightened him witless. Wolves! The thought flashed across his mind even as he looked around for some safe retreat. Of course! Judson had been discussing wolves at the dinner table. He had complained that starving wolves had been attacking his horses, had managed, despite night watchmen, to kill one of his prize stallions. He was promising a bounty for every wolf skin brought to him; he himself would stand watch at his stable that very night. Tobias had heard and forgotten, for he had not intended to take this walk. It had been purely an impulse of the moment.

Tobias leaped onto a log on a rise in the ground, but he realized that this afforded him no protection, so he sprang off and raced to a huge oak that stood at the peak of another small rise. As he ran, he scooped up a long branch which ended in two jagged edges. As he made for the tree, he hefted it in his hand, judging by its weight that he could use it as some measure of defense. Reaching the oak, he tried desperately to scale it, but its very size defeated him. He turned, backing up against the tremendous trunk like a cornered animal, to see three wolves slavering almost at his heels, their eyes luminous in the moonlight, their teeth projecting wickedly from their snarling lips.

Tobias lunged at the wolf in the forefront, shouting as he did so, and the wolf retreated a few steps. But the respite was temporary. The wolves circled, watchfully, biding their moment as the terrified boy fought them off grimly with his makeshift lance. One wolf, seizing its opportunity, slashed at Tobias' leg. Tobias smashed it a stunning blow across its back, knocking the wolf off its feet so that it rolled down the slight slope, yelping in pain and anger. His terror had given Tobias almost superhuman endurance; now, however, he was growing weary. There flashed into his mind a singular thought, considering his situation. If I survive this, he promised himself, let them read me out of meeting. I shall become an artist somehow.

The wolves, sensing the battle almost won, came even closer. Tobias closed his eyes. Just then a shot rang out, and the wolf who had ripped Tobias' leg fell dead at his feet. The others whipped their heads around, hesitated briefly, then vanished into the shadows of the night.

"Thee has come at a good time, Mr. Judson," Tobias called out weakly, but the figure that stepped into a shaft of moonlight was not Judson but a young Indian girl. She examined Tobias' leg while he stared at her in astonishment. Having come to some conclusion, she motioned him to follow her. Looking back and seeing that he was having some difficulty, she returned so that he could brace himself with his arm across her shoulder. Wordlessly she led him east, following a trail that wound its way beside the lapping waters of the creek. Shortly they came to a cabin, even larger than the one that belonged to Judson. The girl took him inside, indicated that he was to sit down near the fireplace, and vanished into another room.

Tobias sank gratefully to the floor. Looking up, he noticed that a broad piece of wood dyed a deep blue had been fastened above the hearth so that it made a generous shelf. On either side of the shelf stood two earthen pots from which vines ran down, decorating the fireplace with lustrous heart-shaped leaves. During the day, Tobias imagined, morning glory blooms curtained the fireplace with a vivid mixture of red, white and blue clusters of flowers. Now the blossoms were closed. How beautiful, he marveled, and promptly fainted.

When he opened his eyes again, it was to see an old Indian woman tending his leg. Feeling his movement, the woman spoke briefly to the Indian girl who came, knelt by Tobias and said, "Have no fear. My grandmother has much skill in these matters."

"I must thank thee for saving my life," Tobias said faintly. "If thee had not been out with a gun . . ." he paused. What was she doing in the dark of night with a rifle in her hands, his mind questioned suddenly. As if reading his thoughts, she smiled and said, "We have been much troubled lately by wolves who attack our horses. I heard them tonight and decided to track them down." Almost as an afterthought she added, "My name is Akomia, in your language 'whip-poorwill.' And this is my grandmother Maconaquah, 'Little Bear Woman.' "

The old woman raised her eyes to Tobias' face when the girl mentioned her name. She stared at Tobias steadily, then rose to her feet and moved silently from the room.

CHAPTER

★ 4 ★

$\mathcal{D}$EAF MAN'S VILLAGE lay east of Peru on the Mississinewa River, that swift-running stream the Indians called "water of many falls," along whose banks in spring the redbud trees bloomed, their tiny purplish-pink blossoms clinging to the branches in clusters like tiny sweet peas, and the dogwoods, with their shiny green leaves a rich backdrop for each cluster of white or pink bracts, marched in a parade of quiet splendor along the river's edge.

Now in June the ground ran riot with color, a carpet of pinks and violets and crimsons, a flower garden that stretched over hills, into ravines and to some utopian horizon not visible to the naked eye.

Before the little group, composed of Tobias, his grandfather, Rowanna Ashton, Le Cateau and Judson, lay some nine miles of riding, a short journey for Joshua Bright after the long and tedious one from Pennsylvania, yet the hardest. What would he find at the end of the trail? Would this be another of those fruitless pilgrimages that always promised so much, only to end, the dream blighted, the bitter taste of disappointment like bile rising in the throat? How many times had a captive woman turned to him, expectancy in her eyes, to have the flood of hope dammed, her misery compounded in Joshua's forlorn glance.

Judson rode with cheery grace, engaging Rowanna Ashton in small commonplaces until, noting her preoccupation, he too fell silent, smiling to himself at the thoughts that filled his mind. On the other side of Rowanna, Pierre Le Cateau whistled a soundless tune. Judson and Le Cateau were both musing about the trading aspects of this trip to Deaf Man's Village; both were meeting Chief Godfroy at his trading post.

The sound of a drum roll broke into everyone's thoughts. Rowanna looked up, startled.

"The Peru Blues," Judson said reassuringly.

"Our cornstalk militia," Le Cateau put in gravely, "led by our fearless Major Loofburrow. You met him on our trip on the *Republican* if you recall, Mr. Bright."

As they spoke, the little group arrived at the field where the maneuvers of the Peru Blues were to take place. The spectators outnumbered the small military assemblage, if it could be called that, for with the exception of Major Loofburrow, the reluctant company

63

STETTLER MUNICIPAL LIBRARY

of some seventy men was dressed in everyday wear. The Major had exchanged the uniform he had worn on the *Republican* for a blue hunting jacket tied with a wide and brilliant red sash. His shoulders boasted epaulettes, and in his cocked hat a tall plume swayed gently in the breeze. The only part of the Major's uniform that Tobias recognized was the large sword fastened near the Major's thigh.

"But what are the men carrying?" Rowanna asked, roused at last from her reverie.

"Guns," Le Cateau replied laconically. "And sticks. And cornstalks."

As one, Tobias and the others reined in their horses to watch the men form a line on the Major's barked order. The men fell in haphazardly, while spectators shouted ribald comments from the side.

"Straighten that line!" the Major roared in a frenzy. Unsheathing his sword, he marched in front of the men, forcing them into a somewhat more even formation. "Pull in that stomach! Button that shirt! Stand up, man! *Stand up!* Straighten your back. This is a military drill, not a corn shucking. You, there Ned! On this field, that's not a cornstalk you're holding. It's a rifle."

"Sure looks like a cornstalk to me," Ned said good-naturedly, examining the stalk as if accepting the possibility that through some mystic power it might have been transformed into a rifle without his knowledge.

The Major passed on down the line, pushing, pulling, commanding, a word for each man, until he had reached the seventieth recruit. He turned smartly, and momentarily was stunned into silence. The line, if it could be called one, had almost disappeared. Men were leaning on their rifles engaged in idle conversation; some had left the line to banter with a few of the spectators; others had hunkered down or stretched out on the ground, ready to doze off.

The Major regarded them dumbfounded, then in a paroxysm of fury, swept his hat from his head and hurled it to the ground. His massive face purpling, he next removed his sash and jacket, unbuckled his sword and tossed them aside. In absolute silence the Major proceeded grimly to roll up his sleeves meticulously. It was only then that he shouted, spacing his words evenly, to the men whose attention he had completely caught by his actions, "Gentlemen! Form a line and keep it, or I will thrash the whole company!"

Under the startled eyes of the spectators, who had been awed into silence by the Major's magnificent raging performance, the men fell smartly into line, and this time when the Major reviewed them one by one, not a man there stood less erect than the Major himself.

"A beautiful sight to behold," Judson said in honest admiration. "Beautiful."

"Does thee think he is a brave man?" Tobias inquired, spurring his horse so he could join Le Cateau as he and the others rode away from the field and the sight of the men now marching and countermarching across it.

"No one could ever doubt the Major's courage,"

Le Cateau replied. "Only his wisdom." When he saw that Tobias seemed puzzled, he laughed and said, "Never mind. I am sure you have other things to think of on a day so bright and promising. As we all do," he added, wondering anew what thoughts so occupied Rowanna Ashton that she rode with them yet not of them, so immersed within herself that she was hardly aware of riding at all.

Rowanna was, like Joshua Bright, apprehensive. She had come this far pursuing what might well be a will-o-the-wisp. She had been visiting in Lafayette when she heard that a man called Jacques du Coeur was planning to establish a school near Peru. Rowanna liked beginnings, new ideas, and she had written to du Coeur to tell him so, to persuade him that a person of her background could be invaluable to him. A while later she had received an invitation to Deaf Man's Village.

She had not lied. Her background was unusual. It was merely that she had not revealed to du Coeur that she had not been happy in her work. How had it begun? She and her parents had come from England to visit a relative in Pennsylvania. Her father and mother had become caught up in a new experimental colony flourishing in a place called New Harmony, Indiana. They had met Robert Owen, the Englishman responsible for a vision of a community where people could live ideal lives, and had found him singularly persuasive. So her parents had gone on with Mr. Owen, and Rowanna had stayed behind with the ailing aunt they had crossed the ocean to see, with the promise that she would join her parents as soon as possible in New Harmony.

The letters had come thick and fast at first, and then slowly. The first letters had been almost ecstatic, the description of the land lyrical. More than three thousand acres of land were cleared around their village, Mr. Ashton wrote, the village itself situated near the Wabash River, backed by the forest on its right bank, and lost in the forests above and below the village.

Mr. Owen was a great man, Mrs. Ashton wrote enthusiastically in another letter. She had heard him speak to a gathering of people. "I do not know how it is" — Mrs. Ashton had scribbled the lines hastily, so that in parts Rowanna had difficulty in deciphering the words — "he is not an orator; but he appears to have the power of managing the feelings of all at his will. Some small dissatisfaction existed among us. A day or two after, Mr. Owen spoke, and it vanished. I am not yet a complete Harmonite, but I am beginning to think that I have caught some of Mr. Owen's spirit."

Mr. Ashton was equally enthusiastic. He had been pressed into service as a teacher. "We are organizing a kindergarten; 'kindergarten' is a German word, my dear, signifying a special kind of schooling for very young children. And we are to have, too, the first free public school system, the first free public library . . . This community is the hammer that will strike the glowing metal to create a new social order. Mark you, my child, sparks will shoot out in all directions. Our town has become a haven for artists, writers, educators, scientists, teachers . . ."

So the months fled by. Rowanna chafed at being trapped in Pennsylvania, yet could not bring herself to leave the kindly aunt whose lingering illness was terminal. But with time the tone of the letters changed radically. In one her father said bitterly, "Mr. Owen is, I think, misled. Be this, however, as it may, I am heartily tired of it; and if I knew how, I would get out of it quickly. The farmers have suddenly become of such importance as to seem to think none of any account but themselves. The hogs have been our lords and masters this year in field and garden. We are now, as we have been, without vegetables except what we buy; and I believe that we shall go without potatoes, turnips, or cabbage this winter."

Mrs. Ashton's letters echoed her husband's disenchantment. "My dearest Rowanna, oh, if you could see some of the rough, uncouth creatures here, I think you would find it rather hard to look upon them exactly in the light of brothers and sisters. Mr. Owen says we have been speaking falsehoods all our lives, and that here only shall we be able to tell the truth. If I am to call these people friends, than I cannot either act or speak the truth."

Her letter went on, and here at last Rowanna was able to perceive her mother's real grievance. "A bell is now rung at half-past five to get up; at six to go to work; at seven for breakfast; at eight for work again; at twelve for dinner; at one to go to work; at six in the evening to return home. If those who are regularly employed are not punctual, they are liable to be reported at the nightly meeting. If they are sick they must have a certificate from the physician! If this is not slavery," Mrs. Ashton wrote passionately, "I know not what it is. I absolutely begin to feel myself a complete slave."

Rowanna had been stunned at these revelations. Nonetheless, when her aunt died, she immediately joined her parents at New Harmony.

Unlike her parents, Rowanna responded to New Harmony. For her it had the flavor of a university town, an oasis of intellectual excitement in a midwest desert arid of thought. There were so many "firsts" here! Robert Owen's oldest son had established a geological laboratory; Thomas Say, a naturalist from Philadelphia, was studying the insects of the area; the French naturalist Lesseur was observing the fish of the Wabash. And the first public speech by a *woman* in the state of Indiana was given in New Harmony! Rowanna, who worked in the kindergarten, would have stayed on in New Harmony gladly. But the great experiment was already beginning to disintegrate. Her parents fled back to England, declaring they had seen enough of America to last them a lifetime.

Rowanna decided to visit with old friends who had settled in Lafayette, Indiana. And then, at long last, she had heard about Jacques du Coeur's plan for a new kind of school. Her friends could tell her nothing about du Coeur; they knew nothing of the man or his background, or even what manner of school he had in mind, since the news had filtered down to them through several people who were vague about the matter.

Yet here she was, uncertain and apprehensive, on her way to a place called quite improbably Deaf Man's Village — how strange such names sounded to one whose ear was attuned to the names of the English countryside. What if her qualifications were insufficient? What if he, as a Frenchman, preferred not to have an Englishwoman teach the children? What if . . .

"Miss Ashton," a voice broke into her musings. "Miss Ashton."

Rowanna shook her head, as if to clear her thoughts, and turned to the speaker. Le Cateau smiled at her gently. "I would not disturb you, except that I think you will not want to miss a most spectacular sight."

The others in the group had already halted, and were staring at a sycamore tree which must at one time have towered so high that it dwarfed all other trees around it. The top and part of the trunk of the sycamore had split away from the main portion, about eighty feet above its gigantic roots. The trunk near the ground was easily at least seventeen feet in diameter and hollow!

Tobias, spotting an opening in the trunk on the northwest side of the tree, spurred his horse on and entered the hollow. The interior was some fifteen feet in diameter. Tobias drew in a breath sharply. The stillness inside the trunk seemed to envelop him. Peering up, his head well back, his gaze traveled up, up, up; the ceiling of this strange cave-like room was

at least eighty feet high. Through large holes bored by a woodland creature into the trunk some thirty feet high, muted shafts of sunlight fell, giving this interior the look of an ancient, abandoned cathedral. Being here, thought Tobias, was like being in meeting with everyone silent, and having the Word of God light his soul within him. Here, in this moment of communion, Tobias felt he could not bear it if he were ever to be read out of meeting. He must guard his thought of wanting so desperately to draw; he must give up his idle and willful pursuit of his own pleasure.

"Tobias, thee must come out," Joshua called, growing restive because the boy was staying too long. "We have a way to travel yet."

Tobias turned his horse, leaving the inner structure of this magnificent sycamore most reluctantly. Rowanna entered, stayed briefly, and emerged again. About to make some quick comment, she caught the look on Tobias' face and remained silent. Joshua refused to investigate the hollow. He could not appreciate the greatest wonders now, he said, begging off. His mind was too heavy with reflection to do justice to what he would see. Perhaps on the way back they would stop there.

Once again the little group resumed its trip. They had gone but a short way when Tobias pulled his horse so abruptly to a halt that Le Cateau, riding behind him, almost collided with him.

"What is it? What has happened? Are you ill?" Le Cateau asked, steadying his horse.

"Look!" Tobias exclaimed. "There. That man on the horse coming this way."

Heading toward them was a solitary rider, advancing at great speed. The man appeared straight, slim and quite tall — if he were standing, he would easily be well over six feet tall. He was a fairly ugly man, but his appearance was so regal and he exuded the air of one so convinced of his own good looks that the physical discrepancy was unimportant. Around his head he had draped a richly figured crimson shawl, in turban style, the long ends falling in graceful folds over his shoulders. His ears were elongated by the weight of silver ornaments that hung in clusters. His shirt, white and embossed with tiny red markings, hung over blue leggings. Topping this was a black frock coat, over which he had flung a wide red silk sash, elegantly knotted and fringed, which reached around his left shoulder, over his chest and under his right arm. His clothing would have been more than sufficient to catch Tobias' eye, but now Tobias found his gaze riveted upon the extraordinary sight of a hog's head strapped to the man's body and blood staining both the head and the rider's clothing.

"Captain Brouillette!" Pierre Le Cateau said, reining in his horse. Judson explained rapidly to the others in the party, before Captain Brouillette drew near, that Brouillette was half-Indian, half-French, the son of a Frenchman who had been captured as a young man by the Indians, and was a most popular man among Indians and whites alike.

Captain Brouillette drew closer, acknowledged the

introductions gravely, and only then replied to Le Cateau's question about the hog's head.

"We are much troubled by thieves," he said, "who steal not only our horses, but our cattle and our hogs. Only this morning I found the head of this hog. Now I am going to Peru to speak to the magistrate. The thieves must be stopped."

"Whom do you suspect?" Judson asked quietly.

Captain Brouillette shrugged. "Perhaps Slade and his men. They are all thieves. Perhaps the white men who have settled closer and closer to our land. All this I will discuss with the magistrate. This," he pointed to the hog's head, "is evidence, is it not? Last time I spoke to the magistrate, he asked, 'Where is your evidence?' "

Rowanna turned her head, trying to avoid glancing at the severed head. Captain Brouillette leaned forward, however, and demanded her attention. "This is evidence, is it not, madam?" he insisted.

"Very conclusive evidence," she agreed faintly.

Tobias sympathized with Rowanna; at the moment he was not certain that his own stomach was up to his looking at a hog's head strapped around a man's middle. Brouillette now turned his attention to Judson, who seemed generally amused at the incongruity of Brouillette's appearance. "You are president of the Horse Thief Detective Association," Brouillette said accusingly. "The Association is supposed to find thieves of all animals, is it not?" Judson nodded. "Then I shall present myself to you and the Association while I am in Peru," Brouillette added, and thereupon he continued on his way with great dignity.

Tobias turned and stared after him, then realizing that the others had gone on and were in the process of fording the Mississinewa where the waters were shallow, rode after them hurriedly. Tobias would have liked to stop and absorb the scene, for the Mississinewa was beautiful, surrounded as it was with flowering trees, but the others pressed on. As Tobias jogged along, studying the land with great interest, it seemed to him but minutes later when Le Cateau called out, "There is the village. We are here."

Tobias glanced at his grandfather. Joshua was gripping the reins so tensely that his knuckles were whitening under the strain. Rowanna Ashton too was ill at ease, running her tongue quickly over her lips as if they had become suddenly parched.

Deaf Man's Village! Journey's end!

CHAPTER

★ 5 ★

TOBIAS' FIRST GLIMPSE of Deaf Man's Village proved disappointing. A few bark huts, crudely constructed, two or three log cabins, and a fairly large log stable stood parallel to the river. Beyond the stable Tobias could see a tall corncrib. The river view from this vantage point was unusually beautiful, for here the banks curved gracefully away into a bend beyond which the Mississinewa gently disappeared from sight.

The trading post itself, set well back from the other structures, was enclosed behind a rude log fence along with five or six two-story houses. To reach the trading post, the little group had to enter by way of a gate wide enough for a carriage to pass through. Inside the trading post, they were greeted jovially by Chief Godfroy, who announced that Jacques du Coeur had not as yet arrived but was expected.

Tobias stared unabashedly, slightly stunned by the mere physical presence of the Chief, who weighed at least three hundred and fifty pounds, quite the most enormous man Tobias had ever seen. Like the other Indians in and around Peru, Chief Godfroy wore leggings. However, the rest of his costume was somewhat different. Godfroy wore a blue calico shirt that fell to his knees in a bewilderment of ruffles that followed one another in such profusion that they seemed to flow like currents in a swift-moving river over the Chief's huge body. When Chief Godfroy turned his head, Tobias could see that Godfroy's hair, which hung in a long queue down his back, was almost completely gray.

When Tobias and the others had entered the room, a young man had risen from a chair and stood by quietly, politely awaiting an introduction. Although his face was serious and composed, the structure of his features gave him a laughing look, helped considerably by the bright happy expression in his blue eyes. His hair was brown and somewhat long, his complexion fair.

"This is my friend, Pepone," Godfroy announced to everyone at large. "He thinks to capture my spirit on paper. Pepone tries and tries but I say no."

The young man grinned. "Pepone is the Miami word for winter. That is my name, George Winter. I am an artist. I have been trying to persuade Chief Godfroy to let me paint his portrait. So far," he added regretfully, "I have been spectacularly unsuccessful."

"You're English," Rowanna said, and then, as if she had made the statement an accusation, went on quickly, "My parents are from London."

"Perhaps we have mutual friends." Winter moved to her side. "I am from Portsea in England, but I spent much time in London studying."

When Winter approached Rowanna, he put his sketchbook down on one of the chairs. Tobias, as if magnetized, gravitated to the sketchbook and studied a drawing which puzzled him considerably. Conversation swirled above his head. Chief Godfroy was describing the condition of the woman Joshua Bright had come to see (two years, alas, wrought many changes: perhaps despair that her family had all died or concern that there had been no word in all that time; Joshua Bright would be able to judge for himself); then, to Judson (yes, he had indeed purchased a group of horses, fine horses as Judson would see; yes, maybe they could effect a trade); to Le Cateau (supplies were again low; Le Cateau could see the stores and assess for himself what was needed at the post; they would rely on him to procure for them whatever was necessary); to Rowanna Ashton (du Coeur would be along at any moment, but if Rowanna wished to wander on the grounds and visit any cabin, she could do so freely; du Coeur would find her, of that she could be assured).

When Winter spoke in Tobias' ear, Tobias leaped and flushed. "Thee must forgive me," he stammered. "I did not mean to . . ."

"Forgive?" Winter said mildly. "But I'm delighted

that you're interested." He pointed to the sketch that had captured Tobias' attention. "I am trying to persuade Chief Godfroy to pose for me, as you heard. So far, I have not been able to do so. I thought I could capture his interest with this. It is a preliminary sketch of a shield."

Tobias stared up at Winter with surprise. "A shield?" It seemed an odd device to use to intrigue an Indian chief.

"Chief Godfroy is descended from a noble of France, one of the great names in that country's history." Tobias turned and looked at Godfroy, trying to visualize him as a Frenchman. "The name Godfroy was famous in French history even before the Crusades," Winter went on. He had picked up a pencil and was sketching as he spoke. "One of his ancestors was Godfroy of Bouillon, who fought the Saracens in the first great crusade. That Godfroy planted his standard in Jerusalem in 1099. Eight days after that heroic moment he was chosen to be king of Jerusalem and protector of Christian interests in the Holy Land. But he refused. He turned down a crown of gold because he said, 'I cannot wear a crown of gold in the city where my Savior wore a crown of thorns.' "

"King of Jerusalem," Tobias repeated. Already in his vivid imagination he was depicting the scene in his mind — the knight in armor in that fabled city, turning his head from the gleaming golden coronet.

"A descendant of that Godfroy came as an explorer to the New World. There is a great mixture of Indian and French blood in these parts," Winter explained.

"And English. But that is a rarer combination. The French who settled in the forts in Indiana, the *voyageurs,* and the *couriers du bois,* the "wood runners" I think you might call them in English, did not draw color lines as strongly as the English did. Godfroy's father was French, for example. Le Cateau's grandmother was Indian. Most of the Indians here in Deaf Man's Village are of mixed blood."

While Winter had been speaking, his pencil had moved deftly across the sheet. Within the shield he had drawn a series of what appeared to be miniature headstones, which Winter described as "vair," pieces shield-like in shape that he had positioned alternately in rows one under the other. The colors, he said, when he filled them in, would represent a fur of blue and silver. The *vair* occupied the top third of the shield. Below the vair would be an arm upraised, holding an arrow. He had no way of knowing what the true coat-of-arms the original Godfroy bore might have been. However, he was sure Chief Godfroy would enjoy ownership of this decorative reminder of his family's grandeur.

While the adults were conversing, a small Indian girl wandered into the room. When she saw Tobias, who seemed closest to her in age, she went shyly to his side. In her arms she clutched a doll which lay staring at the ceiling with glassy blue eyes in a startling white china face. Judson had brought it to Deaf Man's Village on one of his trips to the trading post to examine Godfroy's horses. He had bought the doll in the East and given it to Pitcita, "little sparrow,"

Godfroy's favorite grandchild. Tobias, engrossed in George Winter's conversation, paid no attention to the child, but she tugged at his sleeve until he was forced to turn and see what she wished. She could not speak English, but soon her gestures made it quite clear that she wanted Tobias to mend her doll. The eyes would not open or close. Winter had abandoned his sketch and rejoined Rowanna Ashton, so Tobias led Pitcita to a corner of the room where he studied the doll while Pitcita watched him with large grave eyes.

Tobias had never repaired a doll before, but it was a simple mechanism. He removed the doll's wig, looking up reassuringly when Pitcita gasped. "Do not fear," he said, with a gentle smile, "I will not harm it." He examined the head carefully, found the small piece of muslin that covered the opening, removed it carefully, and discovered the wire that adjusted the opening and closing of the doll's eyes. He adjusted the mechanism, replaced the muslin and the wig. Pitcita's joy was infectious as she ran from adult to adult to show that the vacuous blue eyes of the doll now opened and shut with regularity. She returned to Tobias' side and thereafter clung to him for the remainder of the time that he stayed at Deaf Man's Village.

While Tobias had been occupied, first with Winter and then with Pitcita, another man had entered the room. From the moment he had appeared, Rowanna's attention was riveted upon him. He was an unusually handsome man with broad shoulders and a slender lithe figure. His eyes were an electric light blue of singular intensity that blazed from his copper-tone face. Du Coeur was an Indian, Rowanna thought with surprise; she had been expecting, led to that assumption no doubt by his name, that he would be a Frenchman. She acknowledged to herself, wryly, that she had only been half-wrong.

"Here is Pechewa at last," Chief Godfroy told her. "I think Miss Ashton believed you would never come."

"I was delayed," du Coeur apologized, and added. "My Miami name is Pechewa, which means 'wild cat.' It is not because of my nature" — he grinned at Godfroy when he said this, for Godfroy had burst into laughter — "no matter what he may tell you, but because, when I was younger, I was a great hunter among my people."

So, Rowanna reflected, he identifies himself not with whites but with the Indians. A serious man. Intense. Dedicated. A purposeful man. Rowanna stifled a sigh. Although du Coeur had not spoken more than a few words thus far, she felt she had his measure. He reminded her in great part of Robert Owen and New Harmony. Robert Owen, too, was a dedicated man, and such people swept others either into their orbit or from it. Neither one, she suspected, realized nor cared what effect he had on those around him. But du Coeur was talking. She quickly brought her mind back to what he was saying. He was blunt as to where his interests lay. The school, he said, was still but a dream. It was his dearest wish to establish a school for Indians; true, the Miami had sold their land to the United States government and would be required some few years hence, perhaps five or six, to move to land west of the Mississippi. However, those Indians like himself, François Godfroy and Captain Brouillette, who had white blood, would remain here in Indiana and maintain their holdings, which, he added without false modesty, were considerable.

"Surely there are schools in Indiana which these children may attend?" Rowanna protested.

"Indeed yes. Our children went to a school in Lafayette. The schoolmaster was a fine man — learned, even, which is not necessarily an accomplishment expected of our schoolmasters — but without comprehension. For example, in history, what did our children learn from the white schoolmaster about the battle of Tippecanoe? What did he tell them of our own daring chiefs — White Loon, Stone Eater, Winamac? Or of the Prophet, whose war song rang out from the hills? Or Chief Godfroy, for that matter, a great warrior, a great chief among our people? Did he tell them that the white men, having defeated the Indians in battle, came the next day and burned the Indian village to the ground? No! He asked his class rather if it was not a wonderful thing, this battle, since it then opened a large fertile area for settlement by the whites. Our Indian boys stood up as one in the class. They said, no, to them it was not wonderful. And they left. They walked home from Lafayette, rather than stay in a school that made no effort to understand the Indian mind, the Indian heart." Du Coeur spoke with passion, so strongly that Godfroy, who was about to leave with Judson to show him the horses, stopped and called out in teasing, "Pechewa is making a speech again."

Du Coeur, caught off balance by the interruption, stopped speaking abruptly. Studying Rowanna's expression, he laughed and admitted, "It is a failing of mine. I never mean to make speeches. All I wished was to make you understand why I must build this school, why our children must learn to live in a white world but why they must also live with pride in their people. Without pride, without its own customs, its language, a nation dies, Miss Ashton." Catching her smile, he grinned back. "You see? François is right. I can't hold a conversation. I can only make speeches."

"I am used to men who make speeches," Rowanna replied calmly, once again strongly reminded of Robert Owen and New Harmony. "But I am puzzled. Shouldn't you have an Indian teach your children? With a white schoolmistress, aren't you getting the white viewpoint all over again?"

"Ah," du Coeur pointed triumphantly, "but our schoolmistress shall first learn of our ways. What we need, Miss Ashton, is someone who can belong to both worlds. Are you that person?"

"I don't know," she admitted frankly. "I am open to new ideas . . ."

"New Harmony," du Coeur interrupted. "Which is why I believe you will understand what I wish to do here."

"But New Harmony was a failure after all . . ."

"The experiment failed," du Coeur interrupted once again. "But who is to say if the ideas of New Harmony failed as well?"

Rowanna agreed, remembering a phrase in one of her father's letters: *Our community is the hammer that will strike the glowing metal — sparks will shoot out in all directions.* Who was to know if an idea failed or sprang to life again some future time?

"Come with me, please, Miss Ashton," du Coeur urged. "I should like you to meet some of our children. We can discuss the school as we walk about."

"Discuss?" she inquired with amusement.

"Discuss," he replied firmly.

As they left the room, Pitcita, who had been sent on an errand by her grandfather, entered hand in hand with an elderly woman whom she led directly to Chief Godfroy. The woman, obviously white although her skin was well browned through years of exposure to weather, was small and frail. Her hair was gray, her eyes the milky brown that spoke of cataracts screening her vision. Her fingers were bent and gnarled in hands that trembled slightly; although she was in her sixties, she gave the appearance of much greater age.

"Ah, Mr. Bright," Godfroy said, "here is the white woman you have come to see. She does not speak now. I don't know how you will question her, for I do not think she understands either."

Joshua approached slowly, fearfully. Was this Sarah? She sat in a chair and watched him come, a calm expression on her face. Joshua moved closer, then at last sank on his knees beside her, searching her face, her eyes, for some clue of the little lost sister.

"Sarah?" Joshua whispered.

The old woman placed a shaky hand on Joshua's forehead and ran her fingertips gently across his face.

"Nice," she said. "Nice. Nice."

Tobias kneeled beside her now as well. "Grandfather," he said urgently. Joshua looked at him blindly, tears dimming his vision. "Grandfather," Tobias repeated. "Look to her hands. Thee must search for the crescent moon."

Joshua's heart turned over. This was the crucial moment. He shook his head. "Thee must do it for me," he said huskily. "I cannot."

Gently, Tobias imprisoned the woman's hands in his own. Then, tenderly, he turned her hands so they lay palms upward in her lap.

Tobias kept his head low, then at last turned and looked at his grandfather.

Joshua wet his lips. "Did thee find the mark?" he asked hoarsely.

Tobias shook his head. The palms of the old woman were innocent of any markings. Joshua bowed his head in grief. His own hands began to tremble. Noticing this, Joshua gripped them tightly together.

Pitcita, not understanding, was yet troubled at the sadness of the old man and the boy who had fixed her doll. Suddenly she brightened. She ran and picked up the doll, tugged at Tobias' arm, forcing him to turn toward her. She showed him the doll's eyes, opening and closing, then, pointing to the doll's head and in

turn to the head of the old woman, she made it clear that she wished Tobias to mend the gentle old woman who now sat quietly pleating her skirt, smoothing each pleat as she formed it, crooning the one English word she seemed still to recall, "Nice. Nice. Nice."

Godfroy spoke softly to the little girl, whose eyes filled with tears even as she nodded in agreement with her grandfather's words.

"I have told her," Godfroy translated, "that only the Great Spirit can heal such a one as this." He turned gently to Joshua. "She is not your sister, after all? Not the little lost sister for whom you search?"

Joshua pressed his lips together as he shook his head. Not Sarah. Once again, the quest denied. *Thee shall find our Sarah,* his mother's voice rang in his mind still. *Thee shall find our Sarah. Thee must promise me.* I am an old man, he thought rebelliously. I have followed phantom trails to Canada, to Michigan, to Ohio and now to Indiana. I have earned the right to rest, to go back to my little farm in Pennsylvania and live out such years as are left to me in peace and quiet. *Thee shall find our Sarah. Promise, Joshua. Promise. Promise.*

"What will you do now?" Godfroy asked sympathetically as Joshua rose heavily to his feet.

Joshua shrugged. "I shall continue the search." He turned a sad glance at the old woman, whom Pitcita was now taking from the room, once more hand in hand, chatting in her light quick voice while the old woman nodded and smiled peacefully. "What will happen to her?" Joshua asked.

90

"She is well cared for here," Godfroy replied. "Little Pitcita has a warm loving heart, as you can see."

Le Cateau, who had been absent from the room while the others had been generally conversing, reappeared in time to catch the general drift of what had happened. He crossed quickly to Joshua's side. "Don't despair yet, Mr. Bright," he said quietly. "I know of other white women you may wish to investigate who have lived among the Indians. Indeed, there is one now who lives in Osage Village. When you are ready, I will take you to her."

Tobias motioned Le Cateau to one side and whispered, "Whenever thee can, please take me and not Grandfather to Osage Village."

"You?" Le Cateau repeated with surprise. "But how would you know her?"

"I will know her," Tobias said firmly. "Thee must take me to Osage Village."

CHAPTER

★ 6 ★

H AS MR. WINTER ever told thee the story of the monster in Lake Manitou, the Devil Lake?" Tobias asked. Le Cateau turned from the door of his cabin and laughed. He had gone to see if Rowanna Ashton was nearing the cabin; having heard of Le Cateau's plan to take Tobias to Osage Village, she had asked to accompany them. Perhaps, she insisted, if the white woman there was indeed Sarah Bright, she might be of some help. While Tobias and Le Cateau awaited her arrival Tobias had brought up the subject of the monster. "Mr. Winter said the Indians will not go near the lake, that they fear the evil spirit that lurks beneath the waters. Does thee believe there is a monster in the lake?"

"There is always a monster," Pierre Le Cateau replied, his lips quirked to reveal his slightly crooked front tooth. "Even Great-grandfather wrote of one in his diary, which I may tell you of some time." At Tobias' crestfallen expression, Pierre relented and said, "Since we seem to have time, perhaps I should read it to you now." He crossed the cabin to reach up on a shelf over his bed, from which he removed a well-thumbed book. When he opened it, Tobias could see the fine cramped scrawl which covered page after page in the diary. Le Cateau, seeing Tobias' interest, handed him the diary, but since the language was French, Tobias returned it regretfully. Pierre turned a few pages rapidly but with great care, and then, translating freely as he read, he said: *Today the Indian Aubbeenaubee whose name signifies "looking backward" gave me an account of a creature whom he swears to have seen, a creature sixty feet long with a head three feet across the frontal bone. The Creature, he swears further, is an animal made up of the parts of other animals so that it walks like a tiger but growls like a bear, has a mane like a lion but the tail of a catamountain, altogether a vicious savage beast that attacks men and drags them to its den. Aubbeenaubee wishes me to come and see the creature for myself but I think to do so I should have to drink firewater as Aubbeenaubee calls it, or if he thinks he can play tricks I shall call him the liar he is.*

"Does thee think there is no monster in Lake Manitou then?" Tobias asked, with great disappointment. "Is it a made-up monster, like the one the Indian Aubbeenaubee made up?"

"Ah," Pierre Le Cateau said, "but who is to say if there is or is not such a creature as a monster? Listen. Great-grandfather goes on: *Yet Aubeenaubee may have seen something, for I myself, having been on a pirogue on the River this day with Pipinjakwa whose name signifies "lightning," saw but a stone's cast away a Creature that stood up in the water, a Human of gigantic posture having the face and arms and body of an Indian but leaping up and diving down into the waters showed a tail of incredible size. It may be that I have been in the sun overlong for I could not credit my senses, and when I spoke to Pipinjakwa about the Creature he denied seeing it yet will not be persuaded to return to the river on any account. And so I am perplexed in my mind, for I feel that I may have stayed among these people overlong and take their superstitions as my own.*

Just as Le Cateau finished reading from the diary, a small animal about thirty inches long from head to the end of its bushy ringed tail ran in through the open door. The animal's fur was a mixture of colors — gray, brown and black — and its bright mischievous eyes were surrounded by a black patch which gave it the appearance of having put on a mask. The animal seemed very much at home, for it ignored the occupants and began to play a game with the blanket on the bed, tugging at it with its paws, trying to dislodge the blanket and pull it loose.

"*Voleur!*" Pierre shouted. "Not again! Not twice in the same day." He turned to explain to the astonished but delighted Tobias, "This is my pet raccoon. I call him Voleur, because that is what he is, a thief."

"What does he steal?" Tobias asked, smiling at the antics of the raccoon.

"Anything. He is not much of a specialist, this little thief of mine. For example, this morning when I woke, I looked for my trousers. I reached for them, but they were gone! Where? Why should anyone wish to steal these trousers? I was most perplexed. I distinctly remembered throwing them across this chair when I went to sleep last night. Yet they were gone. I looked all about the cabin, even in the fireplace." He laughed when he saw Tobias' expression. "Yes, even in the fireplace, thinking: did I walk in my sleep, and in my sleep did I wish to add to the fire these trousers which are now so old but so comfortable? Then I remembered Voleur . . ."

"Voleur hid them?"

"Voleur! The rascal! He had pulled my trousers through this crack in the floor." Tobias looked down and saw several cracks in the puncheon floor. "So I had to go under the cabin and retrieve my trousers."

A woman's laughter rang out, startling both Pierre and Tobias. Rowanna Ashton was standing in the doorway.

"How long have you been there?" Le Cateau demanded.

"Long enough to hear the story of Voleur." Laughter bubbled up again, which she halfheartedly attempted to stifle. "I'm sorry," she said helplessly. "But it was very graphic, you know."

Le Cateau grinned. "Also frustrating."

"But thee must put the journals elsewhere," Tobias worried. "They are too valuable for anything to happen to them. Will not Voleur do them harm?"

"Fortunately, Voleur is not literary-minded. And," he added, with a gleam in his eyes as Rowanna reached for the raccoon who promptly leaped from the bed and raced from the cabin, "apparently he is also a misogynist."

"A misogynist?" Tobias repeated, frowning.

"He hates women," Rowanna explained. She shrugged her shoulders and smiled. Le Cateau studied the young woman. She was by no means beautiful, perhaps not even very pretty, yet her warmth and vitality, the vibrancy of expression, the changing color of her eyes, made her appeal unique. To me, at any rate, he added honestly in his mind, for Tobias seemed less happy to see Rowanna than sorry that the mischievous raccoon had disappeared.

"The village is not far, just a few miles from Peru," Le Cateau said, "but I think we should now get started, Tobias."

Tobias had been disappointed in Deaf Man's Village. He was even more so when they arrived at Osage Village. The word village had created a word picture in his mind; he expected to see a bustling, busy area, with many cabins and perhaps a number of wigwams, Indians going about their various pursuits, squaws, perhaps, engaged in making moccasins and leggings, or trimming garments with the silver or ribbons which they wore in such profusion on their dresses, or children playing a game that Mr. Judson had described to him — *yahyouttchechick*, a game similar to quoits, Mr. Judson had said, and then, seeing that Tobias knew nothing of quoits, promised to teach him some day soon — or the Indians at council. When they arrived, however, Tobias discovered that the so-called village consisted of nothing more than a single log cabin and a bark wigwam, enclosed by a pole fence that sagged and in places collapsed completely.

Rowanna, too, was noticeably dismayed.

"But no one lives here," she said, for there was no visible sign of any inhabitant. The silence of decay swallowed all sound. Even Rowanna's voice had taken on a hushed quality. Le Cateau, about to reply, was interrupted by a sudden onslaught of dogs, who materialized from nowhere, howling, barking, dancing around the legs of the horses. Above the harsh yelping of the dogs, a woman's voice rose and dominated the sound, a series of lamentations intermingled with rebuke.

"That is the woman we came to see?" Tobias asked, a worried look in his eyes. Even before he confronted her, Tobias was perturbed. The harshness of her voice, the scope of its penetrability, made him wonder if the search for his grandfather's kidnapped sister was not a mistake. If she were alive, what would years of living with the Indians have done to her? Was it wise for his grandfather to pursue this matter any longer?

Le Cateau dismounted. Rowanna and Tobias followed suit. The dogs leaped around them, accompanying them to the cabin, but running off when the three entered. When Tobias' eyes adjusted from the sunlight to the darkness of the interior of the cabin, he was surprised to see George Winter sitting in a corner of the room, sketch pad in hand. An old woman was berating Winter. He obviously did not speak the language of the Miami, but the woman's message was clear. She did not wish Winter to capture her spirit with his magic pencil. A tall young woman and a short squat man rose when the three entered. They regarded the newcomers distrustfully. Le Cateau explained their mission rapidly. A man of many surprises, Rowanna thought, for he spoke to them in the language of the Miami. Tobias, meanwhile, drew closer to Winter's side, the better to see him sketch, for Winter, disregarding the old woman's scolding, was rapidly filling his pad with deft lines. Looking up, he took measure of the expression on Tobias' face and handed him the pad and the pencil.

"Try it," he urged.

Tobias hung back. "It is forbidden," he said. But almost automatically, he accepted the proffered material. He studied the old woman, who had broken off her stream of complaints as the pad and pencil exchanged hands, her eyes watching every move the others made, and then he began hesitantly to draw.

"Looser, looser, my young friend," Winter said. "Don't grip the pencil like a weapon. Relax. That's it," he encouraged. "Much better. No, no, my boy. Forget details. Fill in the whole picture first. Details

98

can come later, from memory if you wish. Draw quickly. Draw loosely. Draw boldly." He watched Tobias silently thereafter, letting the boy become absorbed in what he was doing. "Excellent," he commented, when Tobias at last raised his eyes from his pad. "A fine likeness. You have great talent, Tobias. You should study art."

"It is forbidden," Tobias replied, his face flushed with excitement. He had made a fine likeness. He knew it. The pencil had flown over the page as if it had life of its own. He had captured the old woman, the small wrinkled brow, the hostile expression of her piercing brown eyes, the sharp nose and tight lips, even the vitality that her age had not diminished.

"May I keep this?" Winter asked, privately deciding that he would have a talk with the boy's grandfather. To let such talent lie idle would be wasteful. With the proper instruction, Tobias might well be a superb artist, even outstanding. That was obvious in this one sketch. Untrained as he was, in spite of glaring errors that needed correcting, the old woman leaped from the page.

Tobias flushed again, this time with pleasure. That an artist like Mr. Winter should ask for the sketch was a great compliment.

Now Le Cateau interrupted Tobias. He had not wished to intrude upon the boy when he was drawing. He too had noticed Tobias' absorption, the communion between him and his drawing, and so had kept his counsel, waiting for the right moment to break in.

"Tobias," Le Cateau said. "I have questioned these two" — he indicated the young squaw and the man beside her — "and they say, yes, she is white. She was captured as a child and has lived among Indians all her life. She married an Indian, a young man called Naswawkee, Feathered Arrow, and these two are her granddaughter and her granddaughter's husband. She does not remember where she lived as a small child, nor anything about her parents. I asked if she came from Pennsylvania, or remembered something about the Quakers" (Le Cateau had called the Quakers 'the men of the black hats') "but the old woman knows nothing. I am sorry, Tobias, but I don't know how you will find out if she is the missing sister."

"There is a mark," Rowanna exclaimed. "Your grandfather said there is a mark by which she can be identified."

"Yes," Tobias said. Then he remembered that the old woman, at one point, had raised both hands, palms outward, to shield her face from Winter's eyes. The palms had been wrinkled but free of any markings. The crescent moon was not there. He had noted this without realizing that he had done so; with a flood of relief, for he had not liked this old woman with her raucous voice and her endless complaints, he recalled the absence of the crescent moon. Grandfather would be disappointed again, but it was certainly better so. "She does not have it," he said. "I looked before."

The old woman was glad to see them go, as were her granddaughter and her husband. Winter rose to go as well. He explained he was not leaving Osage Village yet but was going back further, perhaps to spend some time along the river; there were other sketches of the land he wished to make; the wild beauty of it moved him. Tobias would understand, he added. He could not see it without committing as much as he could to paper.

Rowanna, walking back to their horses, expressed Tobias' sentiments about the village. "It was not at all what I expected an Indian village to be like." She kicked at the grass idly, then, with an exclamation of surprise, bent down to inspect the grass more closely. "Look," she cried. She plucked a tuft of grass and held it up for Tobias and Le Cateau to inspect. Beads glittered on the tough wiry ends of some blades of grass. Le Cateau and Tobias knelt beside her.

"Beads!" Tobias exclaimed.

"Is not this a rich country," Le Cateau teased, "when even the weeds bear beads?" He rose, helping Rowanna to rise as well.

"But what does it mean?" Rowanna asked.

"It is a simple explanation really," Le Cateau began. "Like many mysterious things, it starts with a rational happening. Once Osage Village was a bustling village, but it was razed by white men and completely destroyed. The grass burned, and when it grew again, the blades shot up through the eyes of the beads left behind. As the grass and weeds grew, the beads were lifted higher and higher. And *voilà*, we have grass that grows beads."

The three mounted their horses, laughing. It has

been a pleasant morning, Rowanna thought, one of the most pleasant I have spent for a long time. Tobias' musings ran much in the same direction. He could still feel the warm glow that had suffused his body when Mr. Winter had handed him the sketch pad and pencil. Le Cateau, too, took deep pleasure in the golden glow of the soft summer day; it had clarity of sky, across which a teasing breeze whisked feathery wisps of transparent clouds; the rustling of the leaves was like a sibilant whisper; the Mississinewa rushed by in melodic haste to join the Wabash.

They rode in single file, Tobias first, Rowanna behind Tobias, and Le Cateau bringing up the rear. Suddenly Tobias reined in his horse. "What did thee say?" he called back to Pierre.

Pierre, startled out of his daydreaming, said, "I? I said nothing."

"Did *thee* say 'Ho!'?" Tobias asked Rowanna.

Rowanna shook her head. "I heard it, too, but I see no one about."

As she spoke, a man's voice rang out. "I'll solve that little mystery for you, missy. I said 'Ho!' and when I say 'Ho!' I mean what I say!" Now the man who had spoken emerged from a sinkhole some few yards from the path, followed almost immediately by five men carrying weapons. "Down from the horses," the man said, gesturing with the rifle in his hands. Tobias and Rowanna stared with shock at the group that surrounded them. The man who had ordered them from their horses was about fifty years of age, short and stocky, his bull-like head set forward on his shoulders; his head was clean-shaven on both sides, but thin gray hair ran down the center of it and ended in a limp, skimpy queue on his back. One of his eyes was green, the other brown (Tobias learned later that the green eye was glass).

"Who is he? What does he want?" Rowanna asked. Before Pierre could answer, the man with the glass eye made a mocking bow and introduced himself.

"Old Slade himself! " he said mockingly.

Tobias and Le Cateau slid down; Le Cateau's eyes flashed a message at Rowanna. She made as if to jump down, surreptitiously loosened her shoe, a sturdy shoe with a wicked heel, and then, taking the men off guard, whipped her horse into action, flailing right and left with her shoe. Before the surprised group thought to shoot after her, Rowanna had disappeared around the bend.

One of the men, Rafe Crawley, started to go after her, but Slade called him back harshly.

"Let her go. We don't need her," he growled. "We have the boy."

CHAPTER

★ 7 ★

SLADE HAD CAUTIONED Tobias and Pierre once, briefly, but they had understood he meant what he said. "Make one sound, make one attempt to escape, and you're dead." And he did not speak to them again on the forced march. Checking only to see that both Tobias and Le Cateau were securely bound, Slade swung back on his horse and moved ahead of the line swiftly. (Rafe Crawley had tied ropes around them, sliding the ropes under their left arms and over their right shoulders. "The rope chafes," Tobias had complained quietly. "You don't say," Rafe had replied indifferently.) Rafe held the ropes like leashes on the prisoners, forcing them to run alongside his horse. The horses belonging to Tobias and Le Cateau were led by Snake Eyes, whose name, Tobias thought as he studied the man's sullen features and mean, slitted eyes, was remarkably apt.

They traveled without pause for a number of miles. Suddenly, typically without reason, Slade gave orders that Tobias and Le Cateau were to be mounted on their horses. When Rafe objected, Slade rounded on him with curses. When he gave an order, Slade expected to be obeyed. He didn't have to explain why. It was enough that he wanted something done. Did Rafe wish to argue with Slade? Slade asked dangerously. Rafe subsided, his lips compressed, his eyes filled with hate. Slade laughed contemptuously. Rafe did not frighten him. It had been a long time since Slade had known the meaning of fear, not since those first weeks when he had been captured by Indians when he was still a boy. Yes, he had been fearful then. But he had learned. In time he became more bloodthirsty, more ruthless than his captors. He had led raids against settlers, had razed homes, burned white men at the stake. No Indian struck more terror in the hearts of settlers than Slade himself; it was known that he despised his own people.

It was dark when the swift-moving party came to a halt at last. They had traveled due north, Pierre Le Cateau observed. He knew this countryside well, having hunted and fished in these parts often. He said nothing to Tobias, however, for even if he could devise a means for them to escape their recapture would be almost inevitable. Nonetheless, the thought remained uppermost in his mind.

There would be no food for the prisoners, Slade

ordered, but they were to be allowed to drink some water. Le Cateau and Tobias stumbled to the creek near their encampment; falling flat, they lapped the clear, fresh cool water gratefully. Le Cateau turned his head watchfully and whispered, "Don't lose heart, Tobias. Miss Ashton will surely bring us help."

Snake Eyes aimed a brutal kick at Le Cateau. The prisoners were not to talk to one another, he growled. But Slade laughed.

"Let them talk if they want to. Much good it will do them. We've covered our tracks well."

Le Cateau could probably find his way back, Rafe objected. Rafe had observed Le Cateau as they traveled. This was no city man who couldn't find his way out of a barrel. He was a woodsman, Rafe could tell.

Slade shrugged. True, Le Cateau, whom Slade had met once before, had been a trapper in these woods. But dead men did not return. Rafe grinned. Slade was right. Dead men did not return. Nonetheless, that night Rafe sat on one side of the prisoners and Snake Eyes on the other, rifles handy.

Tobias, lying close to Le Cateau, stared up at the night sky hopelessly. His heart had long since stopped hammering in his body. He knew only a great fatigue and a kind of numbness of spirit.

Pierre looked up at the sky thoughtfully too. He was puzzled. He could not recall that he had ever done Slade an injury, yet he must have, for the memory evidently still rankled. A horse nickered softly. Le Cateau glanced at the animal absently. The sorrel moved restlessly, its red-brown color diminished in the darkness to a muted black. As the sorrel turned its head, a gleam of moonlight painted its face silver. Staring at the sorrel, Le Cateau suddenly recalled the details of his meeting with Slade.

He had visited a small trading post, not far from this area. While he was there, a man had entered. Le Cateau had not known then that the man was Slade. A bag of flour stood on a bench just inside the cabin, under a low open window. Slade's horse had stuck its head in through the window and lowered its muzzle eagerly into the inviting sack. When the horse withdrew its head, it was covered with flour up to its eyes. The horse snorted with disappointment. It looked so comical that Le Cateau had burst into laughter and had turned, grinning, expecting Slade to join in. Slade, however, had gone pale with rage and had tightened his grip on his rifle. Pierre held his own rifle loosely; he had been hunting deer that day. Instinctively he had brought his own rifle up. Slade radiated danger. Two Indians in the trading post froze. They, too, recognized the intensity of this man.

"Who are you?" Slade asked quietly.

"Pierre Le Cateau."

"It's a name I won't forget," the other promised. "And some day you'll have reason to remember that mine is Slade."

Now, lying here on the ground with Tobias at his side, Pierre found it hard to believe that so trivial an incident had brought about this kidnapping. Why the man must be mad, he thought to himself, and then, having conceived the thought, realized that it was so — Slade was mad.

Although positive that they could not sleep, Tobias and Le Cateau did indeed sleep, heavily, without dreaming, and were equally amazed, when Slade prodded them awake, to see the sky lightening and to hear the birds twittering above their heads.

Pierre sprang to his feet. "I've finally remembered where we met," Pierre said. "If you have a quarrel it's with me. The boy has done you no harm. Why don't you let him go?"

"I'll let him go, as soon as the old man pays," Slade returned brusquely.

"Grandfather has but little money," Tobias said. He too had stumbled awkwardly to his feet, his eyes smudged with sleep and weariness. "He is old and not well. Thee should not torment him for my sake. It is not right."

"Well now, my young Quaker, do you intend to convert me to the gospel?" Slade sneered.

"The boy is telling you the truth," Pierre said. "Only a fool would expect to get much money from the boy's grandfather."

Slade whipped around and struck Pierre savagely. "Don't you ever call me a fool again!" He walked off in anger.

"Slade's got that all figured out," Rafe said, smiling. "Judson's the richest man in the county. And the grandfather and the boy are his guests. Judson's a funny man that way. He's got a sense of honor, I guess you might call it." He grinned more broadly.

"He'll never miss the money and Slade's got big ideas for it."

Snake Eyes came by, leading horses for Pierre and Tobias. "You talk too much, Rafe, you know that?" he offered. "Someday you're going to open that big mouth of yours so wide someone will turn you inside out and stuff you in it. Mount up," he continued, in the same flat monotone in which he had threatened Rafe. "We're riding on."

Tobias started to speak to Pierre, but when he caught Snake Eyes' steady glance, he stopped. Subsequently the group rode in silence, Slade once again in the lead, Rafe riding just in front of Tobias and Pierre, with Snake Eyes bringing up the rear.

They continued to ride in absolute silence at a hard pace set by Slade until he called a halt. There, just ahead of them, lay his campsite. A group of men looked at Slade and the others in his party as they entered the camp.

"You've got to hand it to Slade," one of the men laughed. "He always gets what he goes after."

Tobias and Pierre looked around; Tobias, even in his state of shock, was interested in the scene around him, and Pierre was studying the situation, assessing their chances of escape. It was a rough camp composed of a few shacks thrown together haphazardly. At a nod from Slade, Rafe led Tobias and Pierre to one of the shacks, shoved them in unceremoniously and slammed the door shut. It took Pierre and Tobias a few moments to accustom themselves to the sudden darkness. There were no windows. Only feeble light came in through the chinks in the walls.

Tobias sank down wearily against one of the walls. "What will happen to us now?" he asked in a low voice.

"Whatever they plan, Tobias, they won't harm you," Pierre said reassuringly. "They want to sell you back to your grandfather."

"But thee thinks thee will be killed!" Tobias said shrewdly. He struggled to his feet and began to pace restlessly. "Thee must try to escape. Thee must!"

In the dim light, Pierre had been examining the cabin carefully. Finally, he shook his head. He did not know if someone was posted guard at the door, but he assumed it was likely. In any event, the men he had seen milling about the camp were well armed and ruthless. The best he could do would be to bargain with Slade for Tobias' quick release.

The wait for something to happen seemed interminable to both; they took turns pacing. Conversation between them was sporadic. At one point, Tobias asked if there was any possibility that Rowanna Ashton had been able to get help, then had added despairingly that even if she had, it could do them no good for how would she know where they had been taken? Did anyone know about this campsite? They had traveled fast and hard, but Slade had been careful to cover their tracks.

Pierre convinced Tobias that Slade would not permit him to be harmed. Help, he was positive, was already on the way. He sounded more persuasive than he realized, for he himself was fearful that if help did arrive, it would be too late, certainly too late for him. Now Tobias relaxed somewhat and confessed that if he had paper and pencil (and some light!) he would enjoy sketching some of the men, even, he admitted, the man called Snake Eyes. Slade's face, too, Tobias reflected, would be an interesting study. His fingers fairly itched to capture that stony look, and the formidable glitter of the glass eye.

Le Cateau, taken by surprise, laughed aloud. On the heel of his laughter, Slade entered. The look that leaped into his eyes when he heard Pierre's laugh instantly reminded Pierre of the incident of the horse and the bag of flour. This was exactly the way Slade had reacted then. Laughter was a goad that turned him even uglier.

He moved across the room swiftly. Le Cateau braced himself for the blow he knew Slade would deal him. Halfway across the room, Slade changed his mind, turned and slapped Tobias brutally across the face with the back of his hand, knocking him to the floor.

"*Canaille!* Beast!" Le Cateau said through gritted teeth. "It takes a brave man to slap a boy, especially one with his hands tied behind his back."

"I took that and more when I was a boy," Slade replied indifferently.

"Release us. Let me take the boy back to his grandfather, and you'll have my word on it that I'll raise the money you want."

"Release you?" Slade flung his head back and laughed. "Don't you worry about the money. We left a man in Peru to take care of that end of things. But what's between you and me is what we're going to settle."

"With my hands tied behind me?" Pierre mocked. "Maybe you should get some of the others to help you."

Pierre waited, fully expecting Slade to strike him, but Slade surprised him by grinning.

"You just gave me an idea," Slade drawled. The men were bored and restless; Slade had promised them action, but they had seen no real action for weeks. They were beginning to snap and snarl at one another, tempers rising over trivia. Slade pulled the door open and shouted for Rafe. When Rafe came trotting over, Slade whispered in his ear. Rafe slapped his hand across his thigh, and, whooping with laughter, sped back to summon the others. Slade turned and faced Pierre.

"I'm going to cut you loose, Le Cateau," he announced. "You, too, Quaker. And then we're going to go outside and have a little fun."

"What kind of fun?" Tobias demanded suspiciously.

"Why your friend is going to run the gauntlet."

Tobias was puzzled.

Slade grinned. "Don't know what a gauntlet is? It's a kind of sport you might say. Too bad it died out. Why I can remember . . ." his voice trailed off. When he was a boy of ten, he was remembering, back in the year 1795, more than one prisoner had run the gauntlet. The men of his tribe had stood in a double

113

line holding clubs and knives, laughing and chattering, all in high good humor. He would never forget how Sheshequeh would pursue the prisoners down the line brandishing a tomahawk as the prisoners raced and fell beneath the blows, rose again and ran for their lives, their goal the council house just beyond the double line. If a prisoner survived the gauntlet and made it to the council house, he was then entitled to a trial. Prisoners were generally found guilty. Then (Slade licked his lips in retrospect) preparations were begun to burn the prisoners at the stake. Dry sticks and brush were gathered just before sundown and heaped in two circles. A stake was driven into the ground between the circles and tested for firmness. The faces of the prisoners would be blackened, and their clothes stripped to their waists. When they were brought from the council house and tied to the stakes, even strong men cringed and begged to be shot.

As if it had happened but a short time ago, Slade could recall the first time he had applied his torch to the dry twigs. It was Sheshequeh, his adopted father, who had placed the torch in Slade's hands and motioned him fiercely to begin the ceremony of burning. The twigs had blazed. He could still hear how they crackled as the flames leaped from branch to branch. Death to the white man, he had screamed exulting. Death to the father who had run when the Indians had come, who had abandoned his son to save his own skin.

Abruptly, Slade brought his mind back to the present moment. He pulled his knife from his belt and began to cut the cords that bound Tobias. Pierre watched, his eyes blank, busy with his own introspective thoughts.

The gauntlet! In this advanced year of 1840! His great-grandfather had written of it, a practice common among some tribes, that and burning prisoners at the stake. *They take their ayes and noes in this manner,* he had written in his diary. *The council meets seating themselves in a circle after which each man rises and speaks his mind. Thereafter the vote is taken, a heavy blow on the ground with a club signifying death, the club passed from hand to hand signifying life. Counting the strokes, they either condemn or acquit and be they savage or not give a fair trial according to their lights. But the method of execution sickens. Slow excruciating torture excites them. Having witnessed a burning which went from the early evening hour . . .*

Le Cateau switched his memory off abruptly. What a time to be remembering the details which his great-grandfather had recorded so faithfully. Slade had slashed the ropes binding Pierre's wrists. Pierre massaged his wrists, watching as Tobias rubbed his own arms with benumbed fingers. Slade stood at the door, motioning them out. As Pierre approached Slade he said, "I have a proposal to make. If I survive this medieval torture, let's you and I have a duel. Any weapons you choose. If I win, your men allow me to take the boy back . . ."

"No!" Tobias shouted. "Thee must not fight him for my sake. He will kill you."

"That's right, Quaker," Slade said. He shoved Le

Cateau out the door roughly. "A nice neat little duel," he added contemptuously. "All honor and gentlemanly conduct. Snake Eyes," he said to the man who stood waiting outside the cabin, "take our guest to the lines."

The men had already formed two lines, and were now waiting, holding clubs and switches. Here and there a knife flashed in the sunlight. The men were in great good humor, laughing, catcalling, jostling one another. Snake Eyes stood behind Pierre, his rifle at Pierre's back, and pushed him toward one end of the line.

Slade called for two clubs. He thrust one club into Tobias' hands. Then he pulled Tobias along to the other end of the line. "You hang on to that club, Quaker," he said. Then he called out: "I don't want him killed. Just saving that little pleasure for myself," he muttered to Tobias, and watched the gleam of hope that had lit Tobias' eyes fade away.

He signaled Snake Eyes, who pushed Pierre into the waiting double line of men. Raising his arms to shield his face, Pierre began to race through the line as the men, with roars of laughter, brought their clubs and switches down with vigorous whacks. The knives nicked in and out, drawing beads of blood in their wake. Tobias turned his head away.

"No, you don't, Quaker," Slade said. "You watch. It will give you something to think about some long winter night." He seized a fistful of Tobias' hair and kept his head rigid. "Get a good grip on that club. I want you to hit him when he reaches us."

"I won't," Tobias rebelled.

Slade tugged at Tobias' hair so hard tears of pain sprang into his eyes.

Pierre, bleeding and bruised, was now approaching. "Hit him, I say!" Slade roared. He removed his hand from Tobias' head, the better to wield his own club. As Pierre came within his orbit, Slade began to swing. Simultaneously, Tobias swung his club directly into Slade's stomach. Slade doubled over, falling to his knees.

The men stared, momentarily frozen, at the sight of Slade on his knees and the young Quaker boy with the club in his hands.

It was like a painting, Tobias thought incongruously as his eyes swept the scene, everyone standing absolutely still, poised for this brief moment as if some artist had captured it on canvas: the rough-looking men, Slade on his knees, Pierre dazed and bleeding, overhead a brilliant sun, and the leaves of the trees almost too richly green, as if too much pigment had been applied.

Slade rose and seized a club from the man nearest him. "I'm going to finish you off, here and now," he promised Pierre, "and then I'll take care of the Quaker."

Quickly, Tobias thrust his club into Pierre's hands. Pierre hefted it, and waited for Slade to charge him. "It seems we are to have our duel after all," Le Cateau said.

Slade didn't answer but made a sudden vicious swing. Pierre staved it off with his club and then warily backed away a few steps. The men made no attempt to interfere. They prepared to enjoy the fight as a continuation of the sport of the day.

Slade circled and swung, aiming at Pierre's legs. Pierre leaped above the club and brought his own weapon down with great force, just missing Slade's arm. Once again Slade jabbed at Pierre's legs and then brought the weapon up swiftly, delivering a glancing blow at Pierre's arm. Pierre whipped about and smashed out at Slade's shoulder but Slade met Pierre's club with his own.

Slade's men had been shouting encouragingly when the fight had begun but now they fell silent, absorbed. They had no doubt as to the outcome. Slade had dealt Pierre some telling blows; Pierre had come to the fight already bruised and battered. Slade was the stronger of the two and impelled by his madness — die, die, *die*, his mind screamed.

But Pierre handled his club efficiently, poking, jabbing, lashing, avoiding blows when he could, continuing the battle even when he could not escape Slade's drubbings.

Don't let him kill thee. Don't let him kill thee, Tobias prayed silently. It was obvious even to Tobias that Pierre was tiring under Slade's relentless onslaught.

Suddenly Pierre, using his club like a lance, jabbed hard at Slade's stomach. Slade, retreating, stumbled and fell, striking his head against a rock. He lifted his head once to glare at Pierre, then slumped to the ground. Pierre waited, then approached warily. Slade

lay where he fell, his eyes open, spittle dribbling from his lips. Pierre hunkered down and touched Slade's wrist. He could feel no pulse beat, nor, when he placed his hand on Slade's chest, any sign of life.

"He's dead," he said, rising, in a tone of disbelief.

The men moved toward Pierre slowly, their mood ugly, their faces threatening. Tobias ran and stationed himself behind Pierre. The two waited. Suddenly a shot split the air. The men wheeled about, tightening their grips on their clubs and knives. Several started to run to retrieve their rifles.

"Hold it!" a voice called sharply. Jacques du Coeur and Captain Brouillette rode into the clearing, between them the man who had been left behind by Slade to demand the ransom money.

"Run for your rifles!" Rafe Crawley shouted. "There are only two of them. We can take them." Rafe started to cross the clearing.

Du Coeur raised his rifle and shot in the air. Men stepped forward from behind the trees, encircling the clearing, standing quietly with rifles in hand. Not a word was spoken. Some Le Cateau recognized: Chief Godfroy was there, as were a number of Miami and Potawatomi, and French-Indians.

Tobias turned his head; behind him, Alpha Judson leaned casually against a tree, smiling. Spaced on either side of Judson were men Tobias had seen in Peru: Auther Meeks, Asa Martin, Hiram Corn, among others whose names Tobias could not remember. To Tobias' left, Major Loofburrow now emerged, resplendent in uniform, his sword conspicuous by his side. Tobias wondered briefly if the Major went to bed with his uniform on. He certainly seemed greatly attached to it. Nonetheless, Tobias was glad to see the Major and the other men.

Du Coeur dismounted as the rescuers closed in on Slade's followers. Outflanked and outnumbered, Slade's men submitted without a struggle to having their hands tied behind their backs. Their eyes were mutinous and filled with hatred. Herding the men on to their horses, the rescuers moved out in a body, leaving behind du Coeur, who had horses ready and waiting for Le Cateau and Tobias.

Du Coeur walked to where Slade's body lay, regarded it for a moment without expression and then approached Tobias and Pierre.

"Are you hurt?" he asked Le Cateau, seeing Pierre's bruises and the wounds where the blood had dried. Pierre shrugged expressively. Du Coeur nodded. "And you, my son?" he asked Tobias.

Tobias said he was all right and asked anxiously for his grandfather.

"He is expecting you without delay," du Coeur replied soberly, as if Tobias had run an errand and had been overlong at it.

Without a backward glance, the three mounted their horses and rode out.

CHAPTER

★ 8 ★

H UGH PEOPLES, who ran the log tavern on the corner of Cass and Second Street in Peru, had turned over one large room for the court term, a room some eighteen feet square. Against the north wall, Hugh had placed a table around which now, while the court was in session, sat Judge Vawter, the clerk Jim Boice, the prosecutor and several attorneys. Both litigants and spectators crowded the room, spilling over into the doorway and outside. The indictments were only for small infractions of the law at this meeting, but the court drew a crowd nonetheless. Watching lawyers at work ranked above weddings and social meetings for pure entertainment.

Knowing Judge Vawter and his temper, some of the spectators were placing small bets on how long the peace would be preserved in the courtroom. Everyone there remembered the time Jacob Awfield had become a mite boisterous in court, having fortified himself with several drinks before his appearance, and began to argue with Judge Vawter. The judge, a bantam rooster in size with a wattle of skin under his chin which he tugged whenever his blood pressure rose, had snapped out a request that Awfield sit down and shut up until such time as he was requested to speak. Awfield snickered and allowed how he sure admired the little man's spunk, speaking up to Awfield that way; turning to his friends in court, he winked and spat to one side, narrowly missing Letitia Blackston, who promptly whacked him over the head with her bible, which Mrs. Blackston claimed was a "weapon in the hands of the godly." Mrs. Blackston had been ejected from the court and Awfield told once again to sit down and be still, but Awfield grew more obstreperous, whereupon the Judge had risen in his seat and said in white heat, "Jake, I may know little enough about the power the law gives me to keep order in this court, but I know very well the power the Almighty has given me." Whereupon the Judge leaped from his place and rammed his head into Awfield's stomach with a mighty butt, knocking Awfield to the floor. The surprised Awfield was then thrown out by the competent Jim Boice, and court resumed.

Joshua and Tobias Bright were both in the courtroom as spectators, Joshua having been invited by Judson, and Tobias by Catherine Bladen, the daughter of the Judson's housekeeper.

Catherine had knocked on Tobias' door early that

morning, and had entered instantly, catching Tobias unaware in bed.

"Thee must not come in here," Tobias said, clutching the bedclothes.

"Be still, young Tobias," Catherine commanded, pacing up and down his room.

"And I wish thee wouldn't call me young Tobias," Tobias burst out aggrieved. "Thee is only three years older than I am."

"I am eighteen," Catherine flashed back. "I should have been wed when I was your age. At fifteen a girl is more than ready for marriage, but at fifteen a boy is still only a boy."

"Then why didn't thee wed?" Tobias snapped back. "If thee is such a woman?"

"Because," Catherine fumed, "I mean to marry Auther Meeks; I have meant to marry him these past three years; I will marry him if it takes me another twenty. And that is why I am here. I am suing Auther in court today. I want you to come and be my witness."

"A witness?" Tobias repeated, dazed.

"He was at the picnic last week, and so were you. Auther stole a fork that belonged to me."

"A fork?"

"Are you witless this morning?" Catherine cried. "Why do you repeat everything I say? Yes, a fork. You saw that fork at the picnic. You helped me stick the fork into the tree to hold the candle."

"But Catherine . . ."

"But me no buts, young Tobias," Catherine replied.

"If you wish to get up out of bed this morning, you must promise me that you will be in court."

"I will come," Tobias promised, and then shouted after Catherine as she swept from his room triumphantly, "but only as a spectator."

At breakfast, Tobias asked Mrs. Bladen if she knew that Catherine was going to court that morning. Mrs. Bladen replied complacently that she did know, and that Auther Meeks might just as well yield and marry Catherine, or she would hound him seven ways to perdition. Catherine, she added blandly, as she refilled Tobias' plate, did not take lightly to being a woman scorned. She meant to have Auther Meeks as her husband and have him she would. Did Tobias fancy a little more on his plate?

Tobias, clutching his stomach, fled after Judson, who regarded him with amusement. Judson and Joshua Bright were getting ready to ride to court. Judson invited Tobias to jog along with them. He then turned his attention back to Joshua Bright, who was saying that now that Tobias was fully recovered, he and the boy must think of returning to Pennsylvania. Their search for his sister having ended, as always, in failure, Joshua could no longer abuse Alpha Judson's gracious hospitality.

"Nonsense," Judson said instantly. "You must not think of leaving us yet. Certainly not until after the rally."

He was not, Joshua said apologetically, a man much interested in politics. That might well be, Judson replied, but this was to be a fiercely contested election.

125

He was a Whig, as were most people in these parts, supporting General Harrison in his bid for the presidency against Martin Van Buren. Van Buren would not be returned to office, Judson vowed. General Harrison would be the next president, the ninth president of the United States. Things would be vastly different when Harrison was in the White House. Why under Van Buren, only three short years ago, in 1837, the country had been gripped by a financial panic; now they were involved in a senseless war with the Seminole Indians in Florida, which was costing the country millions of dollars and thousands of lives. No, sir, Judson's voice rose, it would be a Whig victory over the Democrats this year, he would lay odds on that. Judson stopped then, and grinned.

"I forgot that you are not a betting man," he apologized.

Before Joshua Bright could form a reply, the three were hailed by another rider who joined them at a fork in the road. Tobias studied the newcomer with interest, for his pockets were spilling over with ropes of all lengths, and several were looped around his belt. He was a tall, powerful-appearing man, with the burning eyes that heralded the zealot.

"Peace be with you, friends," he intoned. "Are you headed for the court by any chance?"

"We are," Joshua Bright replied, his eyes, too, drawn to the ropes.

"I see you studying me," the other said cheerfully. "And I tell you straight out who I be. I'm a thief catcher."

126

Judson laughed. "A what?"

The tall man turned his burning eyes on Judson. "Don't laugh, friend. We are all called to our own work, to our special providences, you might say. All men have been created for some special purpose in this life. They have been set apart for that purpose by the Hand of the Almighty. This boy," he said, pointing to Tobias, "has been set aside by the Lord for a special providence. Do you feel it, boy? Do you feel the Lord moving in you? What's your dream? Your passion? Speak up, boy. Let the Lord hear you say it."

"I sometimes wish to draw . . . very much," Tobias blurted out, semi-hypnotized by the other's magnetic glance.

"Then the Almighty means for you to be an artist."

"Do not encourage the boy, sir," Joshua Bright interrupted. "It is forbidden. We are Friends," he explained.

"We are all friends, and we are all called," the thief-catcher insisted. "What is your passion, brother?"

Tobias, seeing that Joshua refused to reply, said, "Grandfather seeks a long-lost sister."

"He shall find her."

"And what shall I find?" Judson asked, unable to suppress his amusement.

The thief catcher turned, raking Judson's face with his burning glance. He said, then, heavily, "Retribution! I, William Noble tell you that! Remember that name, sir!" He turned his attention back to Joshua. "No one can resist his calling. Not you. Not the boy. Not me. And not this man, who is a horse thief."

127

"Sir!" Joshua Bright exclaimed. "You go too far. This man you have just maligned is Alpha Judson, a man of repute and honor in this community. You owe him an apology."

Judson shook his head. His color had risen and there was a sharp edge to his voice, although he kept up the pretense now of being entertained by William Noble. "Never mind, Mr. Bright. How is our good Mr. Noble to know that I am the president of the Peru Horse Thief Detective Association?"

"And a landowner of considerable acreage," Tobias added indignantly.

"And a horse trader known in many states for his upright and honorable dealings," Joshua sputtered.

"Friend," Noble replied calmly. "He may well be everything you say. But I tell you, and to his face, he is a horse thief. I have been divinely commissioned by the Almighty as a thief catcher. I am diligent in my calling. Let horse thieves, be they any number, be they armed to the teeth, I take them, without weapons other than these ropes you see. I cannot be harmed. I take horse thieves where I find them and tie them and bring them to justice. I have the power, friend. The Almighty has given me the power to look in a man's face but once and know if he is a horse thief or not. I am never wrong."

"Do you mean to try and tie me?" Judson challenged.

William Noble shook his head. "The time is not yet. But I will come for you."

The four riders had come in sight of Hugh Peoples'

128

log tavern by this time. Judson, bidding the others a curt farewell, rode off to join some members of the Horse Thief Detective Association, who were gathered in a small excited knot outside the tavern. They hailed Judson with great relief; would Alpha *believe*, Amos Crume marveled, that during the night some enterprising thief had stolen Judge Vawter's horse. The Judge was fit to be tied. Justice would be short and sweet in his court today, Amos Crume muttered. Yes sir! Short and *sweet!*

"Well, don't worry about it," Judson replied sourly. "We have an expert thief catcher among us, none other than William Noble." Judson jerked his thumb in Noble's direction. "Divinely commissioned, he says. Has it direct from the Almighty Himself."

"Now Alpha, you hadn't ought to talk like that," Amos said uneasily, looking about from one side to the other as if he expected measure for measure from the clear skies overhead.

As Amos Crume indicated, Judge Vawter was in a peppery mood. When Tobias and his grandfather entered, Catherine Bladen was already there. She turned and gave Tobias a brilliant smile, then scowled at Auther Meeks, who was sitting and talking with a man in the far corner of the room. Judge Vawter was talking. Samuel Slater was to pay a fine of two dollars for betting on the forthcoming election. Tecumseh Bartlett was to pay a fine of one dollar for betting on a horse race.

"Which proves," the irrepressible Judson whispered as he found a seat behind Joshua Bright, "that it's just half as bad to bet on a horse race as it is to bet on an election."

Judge Vawter looked around the room with a scowl that called for instant silence. There was an indictment against Hiram Corn for betting on a horse race. Was Hiram Corn in the court? A short stocky man with a balding head and popping blue eyes rose. Had Hiram bet on a horse race?

"Well, it was like this," Hiram told the Judge. "I did bet James Foster fifty cents that my horse Snowdrift could beat little Billy Case running fifty yards." (Little Billy Case, a gangling young man with long legs and a prominent Adam's apple, which was presently bobbing up and down with embarrassment at this sudden tide of publicity, grinned shyly at the judge.) "Well, little Billy can run, I'll say that for the boy, but he's no match for Snowdrift as James Foster ought to know by now. James Foster ought to know, because it was Foster that sold me Snowdrift in the first place. But there you are, Judge. Foster is an ornery man and the only way to prove anything to an ornery man is to PROVE it. Well, I don't want to drag this out, so to make a long story short, it wasn't so much what you'd call a bet as trying to show an ornery man that when he is wrong, he is wrong," Hiram concluded positively.

Judge Vawter pierced Hiram Corn with a cold eye and said a horse race was a horse race, and he could pay the court a fine.

"Twelve and a half cents!" Judge Vawter snapped, preparing to move on to the next case.

"Twelve and a half cents!" Hiram Corn said, shocked. And had another thought. Leaning closer, he said confidentially, "Now, Judge, you oughtn't of fined me twelve and a half cents. Because it warn't a horse race at all, you know. A race between a man and a horse can't rightly be called a horse race, now can it?"

An attorney leaped to his feet. "Your Honor, Hiram Corn is my client. Since a race between a man and a horse is not a horse race, I ask for an arrest of judgment."

"You listen to him, Judge," Hiram said earnestly. "This here young feller's got a heap of learning."

"Twelve and a half cents," Vawter said through his teeth. "Next case."

Another attorney rose to state that Auther Meeks "did take, steal, one table fork, of the value of twenty-five cents, the personal goods of Catherine Bladen, against the peace and the dignity of the State of Indiana."

Auther Meeks was called before the judge and requested earnestly by his attorney to state in his own words the exact nature of the accusation brought against him by Catherine Bladen. Thereupon Meeks, a tall handsome man with dark hair and a thin face which was flushed with earnestness, said gravely that all he had done was to remove the fork from the tree, the candle having burned down, and put it in his pocket, intending to replace the old candle with a fresh one. His attention had been distracted elsewhere and he had simply forgotten the fork.

Catherine Bladen leaped to her feet and blazed, "Auther Meeks forget anything? Ha! Judge, that man *prides* himself on his memory. Any day in the week you can find that man, spending his time sitting on store boxes or in shady places, arguing about such things as law, and theology, or medicine, or phrenology, or mesmerism. Name something. Go ahead, Judge. Name anything—democracy, Whiggery, Abolitionism, temperance—anything, and Auther Meeks will argue the subject. On any side!" she shouted. "And that's the man who says he didn't remember taking my fork? Ha!"

"Catherine," Auther said politely. "The fork had only one tine . . ."

"It did not!" Catherine spluttered.

Auther Meek's gaze fell upon Tobias, who was watching the proceedings with mouth agape. "I have a witness who can testify that I am telling the truth. May I call young Tobias Bright before Your Honor?"

"No, you can't," Catherine said furiously. "Tobias is my witness."

While the two argued, Judge Vawter beckoned Tobias to step up. "Tell me the truth of it, lad," he said kindly.

Tobias swallowed. "The fork did have but one tine . . ."

"*Traitor!*" Catherine hissed.

". . . but Mr. Meeks did take the fork out of the tree and put it in his pocket. As to whether he forgot it was there, I couldn't say, sir, not knowing what was in his mind."

"I see." Judge Vawter turned and stared at Catherine. "I sentence you," he told Auther Meeks, "to be confined at hard labor in the state prison of the State of Indiana for the term of one year." Catherine gasped. Not see Auther for a full year? She turned upon Judge Vawter like an avenging fury.

"That's ridiculous," she cried. "I won't have it."

"Jim," Vawter said to his clerk, "kindly remove this hysterical young woman from the court."

Boice advanced upon Catherine firmly. She retreated before him, shouting that she would bring this case before the highest courts, she would never permit sentence to be carried out . . . Her wailing voice could be heard dwindling away as Boice calmly put her out of the court room.

Auther stood straight as an arrow before the Judge, who had motioned him to remain where he was. Now the Judge sighed. "Sentence suspended." Meeks grinned and started to leave. "Not so fast, young feller," the Judge snapped. "I find you guilty of taking that young woman's fork. You will return the fork, or failing that, pay her the sum of twenty-five cents. Further, you will pay this court a fine of twelve and a half cents. Next case."

The attorney who had represented Hiram Corn now rose again. His client, Martha Jennings, did accuse James Pettit, the said James Pettit, not having the fear of God before his eyes, and being moved and instigated thereunto by his satanic majesty, the Devil, did then and there wickedly, unlawfully and feloniously steal, take and carry away a knife belonging to

134

Martha Jennings, an heirloom left to her by her English grandmother . . .

Judge Vawter closed his eyes and his head nodded while the voice of the attorney droned on. This case duly disposed of, the final dispute before the court involved a quarrel over a horse.

Asa Martin claimed he had found a horse belonging to him on Judson's property, to wit, in Judson's stable. The horse was fifteen hands high, brown in color, no white markings of any kind, with an identifiable scratch near his hip. That scratch, Martin swore, had been caused by the sharp root of a tree that Martin had blown up. The horse had sustained the injury while Martin had been plowing in the field.

"Your Honor," Asa said, "I taught that horse when he was still a colt to lean his ears when I pointed a finger at him. You run that horse out on a field, you'll see he moves at kind of a shuffling pace. A man knows his own horse, dammit," he shouted. "And I say Alpha Judson is just a thief. I don't know why he wants my horse. He's got more than enough of his own. But I say that's my horse, and I say Judson ain't goin' to have him."

"Shame!" several voices cried, but others called out, "Asa's telling the truth. That there is his horse, like he says."

The Judge called sharply for order in the court. He then asked Judson to take the stand. Tobias and Joshua leaned forward to catch every word. They had been appalled and shocked to hear a fellow townsman speak out against Judson with so serious a charge.

Judson smiled at them, and looked around the court room, relaxed and pleasant in manner.

The horse was indeed fifteen hands high, brown in color, no white markings of any kind, and with an identifiable scratch near his hip, Judson agreed readily. However, his good friend Asa Martin was mistaken.

"That scratch, Your Honor, was made by a nail in the stable door. As for the lean of the ears, my horse contracted that when he was a colt. And as for the pacing, the horse has a slow gait. I have several slow-gaited horses in my stable, Your Honor, as I can prove. I could call at least twenty witnesses or more who could testify to that, sir."

"How long have you had the horse?" Judge Vawter asked.

"Seven years."

Asa Martin shot up out of his seat. "That's a lie. That horse is no more than five years old."

Judson turned to face Martin. "Asa," he said earnestly. "I know you've somehow convinced yourself that I've got your horse. I don't know why. But we've known each other too long to quarrel like this. We're fellow members of the Horse Thief Detective Association. If we don't set a good example for our neighbors, who will? Judge," he said, turning to Vawter, his hand outstretched in an appealing gesture, "Anyone here can tell you that I've more horses than I know what to do with. Buying, trading and selling horses is my business. I'd like to give

136

Asa this horse and call this whole sorry thing off."

"Give me my own horse. *Give* me my horse!" Asa Martin was beside himself with rage.

"Do you want the horse?" Judge Vawter asked Martin.

"You're damn right I want that horse," Asa swore.

"Case dismissed," Judge Vawter muttered. He rose. "Everybody rise," Jim Boice shouted. The judge moved briskly out of the room without a backward glance. He was hungry and tired.

The crowd filed out, agreeing that this day's session in court had been one of the best so far. Opinion was divided, some holding that Asa Martin had come off real well, getting a horse free like that through Judson's generous gesture, others muttering that there was probably more here than met the eye and where there was smoke there must be fire.

Asa Martin, coming face to face with Judson outside the court room, said, "I'm gonna nail your hide to the barn door one of these days, Alpha."

"He is a wicked man," Tobias said to his grandfather, "to speak to Mr. Judson that way."

Joshua was perplexed. He could not understand how anyone could attack a man of Judson's honor and reputation, and was saddened to think that many in the crowd were ready, even eager, to believe the worst.

Rowanna Ashton, who had slipped into the courtroom to hear the final case, now approached the Brights quietly. Her face was downcast; her eyes troubled. She said to Judson, who had joined the

Brights, "May I speak to you alone for a moment, Mr. Judson?"

Judson stepped aside obligingly. Rowanna spoke quietly, but Tobias, whose hearing was extremely acute, overheard.

"Mr. Judson," Rowanna said. "I examined the horse you gave to Mr. Martin, meaning to step forward as a witness for you if you should need an expert."

Judson raised his brows. "An expert?"

"Don't play the fool with me," Rowanna said sharply. "I've lived around horses all of my life. We raised them in England. I checked that horse's teeth. Mr. Martin was telling the truth. That horse is no more than five years old."

The meaning of what Rowanna was saying sank slowly into Tobias' consciousness. She was accusing Mr. Judson . . . it was unthinkable. Suddenly the burning glance of William Noble seared Tobias' memory. Mr. Noble had said: *The Almighty has given me the power to look in a man's face but once and know if he is a horse thief or not.*

"You are mistaken," Judson replied easily and laughed. "You don't know Asa Martin. Why he'd complain if you hung him with new rope. In any case, he has the horse. Why bother your pretty little head about such matters?"

Rowanna drew a deep breath. "I bother," she replied slowly, "because I think . . ." she stopped and could not go on.

"That I am a horse thief? Does that make any sense at all?"

"No. And that is why I am so puzzled, why I felt compelled to speak to you."

"And so you have, my dear. And I appreciate your concern. I am glad you honored me with your confidence."

Rowanna looked at Judson uncertainly. She could not have been wrong about the horse. She was positive. But perhaps Judson hadn't remembered how long he had had this particular horse. After all, he did own so many. Had she the right to accuse when she had no proof other than this slight slip regarding the horse's age? If Judson were a thief, would he stand there so assured, so pleasant and charming in manner, listening so courteously to so terrible an accusation? "I'm sorry," she said haltingly. "I had no right . . ."

"Please," Judson reached and took her hand in his own, pressing it gently. "Please. It distresses me to see you so unhappy."

Tobias turned to mount his horse, preparatory to the ride back to Judson's home. On the way back, he was lost in thought. Judson had explained. The matter rested. Or had he explained? Tobias' thoughts were a whirlwind of confusion.

When they were halfway home, Tobias blurted suddenly, "Grandfather, I think we should go home."

"We shall, Tobias, we shall," Joshua agreed instantly, "as soon as the rally is over."

"Must we wait for the rally?"

"I promised Mr. Judson," Joshua replied. Tobias was silent. If his grandfather had promised, then they could not leave at once. Grandfather was a man of his word.

CHAPTER
★ 9 ★

*J*UDSON HAD TAKEN TOBIAS, with his grandfather's permission, to the great Whig rally that had been held on the site of the battleground of Tippecanoe. It was a sight, Judson had urged, that Tobias was not likely to see again; true, Judson proposed to hold a rally on his own grounds, but it would in no way be as colorful or exciting. The boy would soon be returning East, Judson argued; he had had a difficult time during his visit. Judson would like, somehow, to make it up to the boy. Judson's open, easy manner, his courtesy, his charm and sincerity were not to be denied. In the end, Joshua agreed that Tobias might go.

George Winter, having heard of the proposed trip, gave Tobias a sketch pad. "You must sketch, sketch,

sketch," he advised, "until the pencil feels like an extension of your fingers."

There had been much to see; people, by the thousands, converged upon the battlefield, by land and by water, in every conceivable kind of transportation. Some arrived in canoes gaily decorated in Whig emblems; others took steamers from Lafayette to a landing on the Wabash a mere two or three miles from the campsite. By wagon, on horseback, trudging on foot (one enterprising pioneer had mounted his small cabin on wheels, yoked it to oxen, and had arrived in grand style), the multitudes poured in.

Judson took Tobias to the site where the men who had fallen in that fierce battle between General Harrison's troops and the Indians were buried. It was a small space enclosed by a nondescript wooden fence. There were no markers. Studying this oasis of silence in the tumult around him, Tobias felt suddenly saddened; he sat on the ground and quietly began to sketch. Judson waited patiently. When Tobias was finished at last and rose, Judson said nothing but pressed his hand on Tobias' shoulder.

"Hungry?" Judson then asked lightly.

Tobias grinned, his mood changing.

"I'm always hungry," he admitted candidly.

"Good. Let's see what we can find."

Together, the man and the boy strolled past several lunch wagons, which were doing a thriving business. Tobias looked up at Judson inquiringly; the aromas assailed his nostrils and he took a deep breath hopefully.

"Just be patient. I promise you some real food," Judson said.

Everyone else seemed headed for the real food, too, Tobias thought, as streams of people, laughing, talking, arguing amiably, moved along with them.

"Where are we going?" Tobias asked.

"To the barbecue." Judson pointed. A few feet away, there was a long trench, in which fires burned, crackling, leaping to embrace the spits on which whole carcasses of oxen and sheep, interspersed here and there with shoats, were being turned.

"What will it be?" one of the carvers called out to Tobias, holding his long sharp knife ready to serve whichever part Tobias might fancy.

"Want to start with the burgoo?" Judson suggested. Behind the barbecue trench, huge kettles were suspended over slow burning flames, and women were busily ladling the thick, highly seasoned soup into outstretched bowls.

"I don't know what burgoo is," Tobias confessed. "But it smells like . . . mmmmmm . . ." Tobias was at a loss for words.

The burgoo, Tobias soon discovered, was more like a stew than a soup, so thick he could not drink it but had to chew away at the morsels of food that he spooned up—bits of chicken, a variety of vegetables, a number of kinds of meats and small game he could not identify.

"Save room for some of the barbecue," Judson advised Tobias with a laugh, for Tobias was now wolfing down corn cakes as well.

A group of elderly men, dressed in uniforms that looked strange to Tobias, went by, chattering among themselves.

"Veterans," Judson explained. "They fought here with General Harrison back in 1811. Not many of the old-timers left anymore." He saluted the men gravely; gravely they returned it. Tobias caught snatches of their conversation as they passed him. "Remember after the fighting how we burned down that Indian town, cornfields n' everything . . ." "People today, living nice and peaceful, they don't know what it was like back in them days . . ." "Murdering savages, the whole lot of them . . ."

The men moved on, the reminiscences eddying in Tobias' mind like ripples in a freshly disturbed pool.

There had been speeches, many speeches, to which Tobias listened at first and then lost interest; there had been music, too, bands marching around the field, and a band on the grandstand from which the speeches were hurled at the crowd.

It had been a wonderful, interesting, exciting day, and one that Tobias would long remember. And now there was the rally on Judson's property to look forward to. There would be a barbecue, and music, and speeches, Judson announced, but Tobias was not to expect it to be so grand as the rally held on the battlefield.

Tobias, lying on his bed and staring dreamily at the patches of moonlight that patterned the wall in his room, thought sleepily about the rally to be held the next day. His eyelids began to droop; I better get up

144

and get undressed and go to bed, he thought, too lazy to rise. Suddenly sleep fled; wide awake, he shot up out of bed and said furiously, "Thee must not come into my room . . ."

"Shhhhh!" Catherine Bladen hissed imperatively. "Be quiet!"

Tobias opened his mouth to object to her high-handed manner but she leaped across the room and placed her hand across his lips. "I need your help," she said. "It is a desperate matter. Come at once, but don't make a sound."

Obediently, Tobias tiptoed down the steps behind Catherine. Outside, she gave him no chance to question her. When he began saying "Is someone injured? What . . ." she rounded on him, declaring fiercely that he was not to make a sound, not a single solitary sound, spacing out the words like a military command. She led him swiftly, finding her way easily along the moonlit trail. When it seemed to Tobias they had traveled miles, she came to an abrupt halt. They were standing near a deep hole filled with water. Frogs kept up an insistent croaking, a series of deep-throated calls that echoed and re-echoed in the stillness of the night. Not far from the water, Tobias could see a cabin.

"Stay here," Catherine ordered and vanished into the darkness. Tobias waited, puzzled, meanwhile staring at a slab of wood which someone had carefully placed over the water. He drew closer, then, on impulse, stepped onto the plank and tried to peer down.

"Pssst." Catherine had materialized again, holding

145

a saw. "Tobias," she whispered. "Come here, and bring the plank with you."

"Bring the plank?"

"You are a very tiresome boy," Catherine snapped, but remembering to keep her voice low. "I've never met anyone so set on repeating things. Yes. Bring the plank. Now saw it. Saw it, I say," she ordered, as she thrust the tool into Tobias' unwilling hands. "And don't cut it all the way through."

"I won't," Tobias said stubbornly. "If thee wishes this sawed, then thee must do it. Whose cabin is this?" he asked, suddenly suspicious.

"Auther Meeks. It's just a practical joke," she said hastily. "I promise you that Auther will not be hurt. I don't want to hurt Auther," she added impatiently, as Tobias still stood irresolute. "I want to marry him."

"Thee chooses a strange way to win a man," Tobias said. But seeing that she was implacable, and would give him no peace until he did as she asked, he began to saw the plank, slowly moving the tool back and forth, stopping to listen, even as Catherine was listening, for any sound from the cabin beyond.

A practical joke, Tobias mused. These two, Catherine Bladen and Auther Meeks, were really more alike than they realized. Auther Meeks was himself a practical joker, as Tobias well knew. When Tobias had been in the village one morning, he had met Auther standing outside the general store, looking for all the world like its proprietor, leaning up against one of the several posts that held the overhang above the store. Auther had hailed Tobias, who had stopped to pass the time of day with him. As they were talking, a man rode up, dismounted, hitched his horse and inquired politely, "Can you tell me where I can find Lawyer Tibbs?"

Auther said just as politely, "Why, sir, your first guess is a lucky one. Lawyer Tibbs has his office just above." He pointed to an open window which fronted the street.

The stranger thanked Auther for his courtesy and entered the store. Anson Crowell, who owned the shop, was, as it happened, upstairs at that moment talking to Lawyer Tibbs, having gone upstairs by the only available means, an outside wooden stairway behind the store not visible from the street or the store. The stranger came out, looked puzzled, and addressed Auther once again.

"How do I get up there?" he asked plaintively. "You don't have steps going up anywhere in the store."

"That's the truth," Auther replied gravely. He motioned to the post. "You'll just have to do what everyone else does. Climb up this post to the little roof and go in through that open window."

The man stared at Meeks, then made up his mind. "If you'll give me a boost?"

Meeks was most obliging. He helped the stranger up the post, while Tobias watched, his eyes brimming with suppressed laughter.

Lawyer Tibbs and Anson Crowell, sitting at ease in Tibbs' office and discussing politics, stared in utter astonishment as the stranger climbed in through the window.

"Here now," Lawyer Tibbs exclaimed, "what's all this about?"

"Simon Swope asked me to give you these papers you wanted, as long as I was headed for Peru anyway," the stranger explained. He dug into a pocket, withdrew several sheets of paper and laid them on Lawyer Tibbs' desk. "Simon's by way of being a neighbor of mine," he added, since Tibbs and the other man were both looking at him rather strangely. He lifted his hat politely, and while the two men watched open-mouthed, climbed out the window again, walked gingerly down the roof and slid down the post. He unhitched his horse, muttering meanwhile to Auther, who watched him with an innocent expression, "It appears to me that friend Tibbs can't do too much business. He makes it mighty hard for a body to get to him."

"Well, I guess you might say it is hard," Meeks answered solemnly, "but folks around here don't even notice it."

The man rode off, and now at last Auther and Tobias burst into laughter.

"Thee shouldn't have done that," Tobias sputtered.

"It was only a little prank, lad," Auther grinned. "Little pranks help keep a man's mind hopping. Keeps him from getting too set in his ways, you might say."

As Tobias worked on the plank, he wondered how Auther Meeks would respond to being on the receiving rather than the giving end this time.

"That's enough," Catherine whispered, breaking

148

into Tobias' thoughts. "Now, place the plank back across the water. The other side! Put the cut side down. That's it. How does it look?" She leaned over and inspected it carefully. "That should do it," she said with satisfaction. "Tomorrow when Auther comes to get water he'll be begging for help."

Catherine took the saw and melted into the darkness again. "We can go now," she said, when she returned. "Now don't fret about Auther. I'll come back in the morning and see that he gets out of the well all right."

Suddenly she froze. "Quick, hide. I think we woke him." She dragged Tobias into the shelter of some underbrush, from behind which they peered out and watched Auther Meeks who came cautiously along the path, gazed around, cocked his head to one side, listening intently. The frogs, having stopped their serenade when Tobias and Catherine had been fussing with the plank, were now in full vigorous cry again. Apparently Auther was satisfied that all was well. He nodded his head, started to go back to the cabin, changed his mind, turned and went to the well, where he stepped boldly on to the freshly-sawn slab. The slab promptly gave way, and Auther Meeks landed in the water, immersed to his armpits, trapped by the board in such a manner that he could not sink but could not extricate himself either.

When he began struggling, Tobias made as if to rush to Meeks' assistance, but Catherine gripped him firmly, shaking her head. After a bit, Meeks began to shout for help. Presently he subsided, resigning himself to spending the rest of the night in the water. At least, he consoled himself, it was a warm summer night, and the water was not cold. Uncomfortable, he concluded, but not completely unbearable. Now Catherine stepped from behind the bushes, pulling Tobias along with her.

"Why, Auther," she said sweetly. "You bathe at strange hours. And in strange places. But Tobias and I mustn't disturb you. Come, Tobias, we must continue our little stroll."

"Catherine," Auther shouted. "You did this to me. When will you let me be?"

Catherine turned. "When we are married," she said.

"Why me?" Auther Meeks moaned.

Catherine considered the question thoughtfully. "I really don't know," she answered finally. "I've seen better looking men. You're lazy. You'll never give me any of the things I want. We'll spend our lives battling. I could make a list as long as my arm, probably. But I love you. And if you could take the time to think about it, I'm the most exciting woman you'll ever know. There's no use appealing to Tobias to help you get out," she added, catching his glance. "It was Tobias who sawed the plank in the first place."

"That's not fair . . ." Tobias began, but Auther interrupted.

"Catherine, my love," he said, "do you want your husband wet or dry?"

Surprisingly, Catherine burst into tears. She rushed to the well and, disregarding Meeks' precarious position, kissed him, her tears wetting his face and giving their first kiss a salty tang, an augury, Meeks thought with resignation, of their life together. He kissed her back, now that he was committed, with zest, until Tobias, standing awkwardly by, cleared his throat with embarrassment.

Catherine lifted her tear-stained face, her eyes glowing. "Help me get Auther out of the water," she said.

When they had freed him, Catherine turned to Tobias. "Can you find your own way back?" she asked hopefully. "I must see to it that Auther gets into dry clothing."

Tobias nodded. He watched Catherine and Meeks walk back to the cabin, arm in arm, shrugged his shoulders, and began to run back the way he had come.

When he was within sight of Judson's cabin, he lingered, wide awake, unwilling to go back to his room to sleep the night away. Before him the land lay quiescent in the moonlight, the ravine sloping behind the cabin a hollow of deep shadows, the stable beyond it etched gray-black against the starred sky. All the world slept; only he was abroad, alone but not lonely, his senses honed somehow to every movement, every whisper of sound, spectator and participant in the night's solitude, at one with the hidden creatures of the woods scurrying through the quiet hours until dawn would coax them to rest. A wind had sprung up, gentle, soft, undemanding, delicately fingering the leaves above Tobias' head.

Tobias glanced up and then let his gaze wander back to the ravine, idly, and once more to the outline of the stable. Frowning, puzzled, he swiveled his glance back to the ravine. Had he caught a glimpse of something, some furtive movement, or had he just imagined it? The darkness there in the ravine was opaque; nothing stirred. Yet Tobias felt disturbed. His mood broken now, he turned to go to the house, and turning, caught sight peripherally of a horse rising slowly, ghost-like, from the ravine, led by a solitary figure, who moved like a wraith before the animal. Momentarily, horse and man moved across the land through a shaft of moonlight, the light mane of the chestnut mare silvered by the moon, and then they were swallowed by the shadows again.

Tobias was tempted to run to the house, to wake Judson and warn him . . . of what? Perhaps he had better wait before he roused the household. As quietly as he could, Tobias moved down toward the ravine, hugging the shadows, although the man did not turn once but continued on down the path worn packed and hard by Judson's horses, through the ravine, up again and close to the stable. Everything was in darkness. Tobias could not make out where the man had gone. Horse and man had vanished, perhaps somewhere inside the huge stable. Then the sound reached him; the horse whinnied softly, the man's voice soothed, the horse fell quiet.

Then it was all right, Tobias sighed with relief. It was only Judson. Tobias had recognized his voice even though the words had been brief. Yet a sense of uneasiness still tugged at him. Tobias determined to follow the direction of the voice which had seemed to come from behind the stable. Tobias slipped around to the back silently and realized with a shock that the stable, built on a hill, rested not on solid ground but on a lower level dug into the hill, a cavern whose entrance was hidden by a heavily overgrown thicket of trees. Tobias moved closer and peered in. Judson was removing burlap sacks from the hoofs of the horse, meanwhile talking to it in a language the horse seemed to understand, for it was obedient to his touch and was quiet. In a few moments, Judson was finished with his task. He stood in the doorway a moment, studying the animal in the cave, and smiled a warm happy smile that lit his face. Then, having obscured the opening with brush, he melted into the shadows.

Tobias could feel his heart thudding against his rib cage. The meaning of what he had seen was clear; he had recognized the mare, a high stepping animal with a graceful arched neck, golden chestnut color and a diamond-shaped mark on its forehead. The last time Tobias had seen this horse, Jacques du Coeur had been riding it.

Tobias sank to the ground, overwhelmed with misery. So the mysterious horse thief was Alpha Judson after all — friendly, humorous, understanding Judson. Tobias wished desperately that he and his grandfather had never begun their search for the crescent moon. If they had not, he would still have been in Pennsylvania, and not confronted with a situation he did not know how to handle. Groaning, Tobias buried his head in his hands.

CHAPTER

★ 10 ★

$\mathcal{T}$HE DAY OF THE RALLY at Judson's was clear, bright and sparkling with sunshine diffused now and then by small woolly clouds that drifted in quiet ripples across the sky. It was not so exciting nor as big as the rally Tobias had seen at the Tippecanoe battlefield, yet it was well attended, people having come from miles about to hear the speeches, listen to the band and partake of the fixings. Mrs. Bladen and Catherine seemed to be everywhere at once, mother and daughter both competent, and Catherine, now that she was definitely affianced, charming and affable. Tobias was pleasantly surprised by the change; Auther Meeks seemed completely devoted, running to do her bidding whenever she sought his help.

Tobias could hear Pierre Le Cateau, who had leaped up upon a wagon that was sheltered in the shade of a huge maple. Faces were upturned, smiling, for Le Cateau was discussing the incumbent president, Martin Van Buren. "Friends," Pierre said, "we expect the president of the United States to live well. But we do not necessarily wish to see the Little Magician turn the White House into a palace." The crowd laughed good-naturedly. Van Buren was known by many names; he was sometimes called the Little Magician, the Kinderhook Wizard, or the Fox of Kinderhook, names which had come about because as a boy of fifteen, Van Buren had already been a law clerk for a full year in Kinderhook, New York, and had helped win his first lawsuit. "However, if the rest of us can manage with spoons made out of tin, or horn, or wood, I think gold spoons in the White House are too much. Now if it was royalty we had in Washington, maybe we could accept gold spoons. But even as you and I, friends, Van Buren was just a farm boy before he rose to the highest post in the land." Pierre paused, turning his head from one side to the other to scan the faces of the people before him. Then he leaned forward confidentially, "Now I hear tell they're planting mulberry trees in the White House garden. Next thing you know they'll be importing silkworms so the president can have silk woven into cloths and napkins for the presidential table."

"You tell them," a man in the crowd called out, grinning.

"At that I guess we could live with extravagance in the White House," Pierre went on, his voice taking on a graver tone. "What we cannot take, and what we have had under a Democratic administration, are financial panics. We cannot afford a 'hard times' president, my friends. That is why this country will make a change in the election, why you and I and other Whigs throughout the nation will put a man in the White House who has experience with government, a man, I will remind you, whose every thought was for the little people, a man who, as the first delegate from the Northwest Territory to the United States Congress, pushed a bill through so settlers with not much money but the will and the determination to carve homes for themselves out of the wilderness could buy land at prices they could afford. I'm talking about William Henry Harrison . . ."

"Tippecanoe and Tyler, too," another man shouted.

"That's our slogan," Pierre Le Cateau agreed. "It's the slogan that will carry William Henry Harrison, old Tippecanoe himself, right into the White House. A man like you and me, not too proud to live in a log cabin, and not too fancy to be above drinking hard cider with the rest of us."

"Break out the cider!" a third man whooped. "Let's drink to a Whig victory in 1840!"

Tobias felt a hand lightly touch his shoulder. Whipping about, he was greeted by Rowanna Ashton, who had come up behind him during Pierre's speech.

"He's quite good, isn't he?" she whispered.

"He talks a lot," Tobias said candidly.

Rowanna burst into laughter. "An absolute must," she assured Tobias, "for anyone who has political ambitions."

Tobias regarded Pierre with renewed interest.

"Does he have political ambitions? I thought Mr. Le Cateau wanted Mr. Harrison to be elected."

Rowanna laughed again. "Oh, Tobias. He doesn't want to be president of the United States. Not yet, anyway! No, he is running for State Senator. Haven't you heard any of his speeches?"

"Speeches, Miss Ashton," said a voice behind her, "tend to inflame the hearers, present as the truth only those facts the speaker wishes to reveal . . ."

"Mr. Bright! Have you been here all this time?" Rowanna asked. Joshua Bright nodded. "And whom do you support in this election?" she continued.

Joshua made a small gesture of indecision with his hands. "However I decide, Miss Ashton, it will be, as in all political affairs, for reasons based upon principle."

"Cromwell said he 'could neither win the Quakers by money, nor by honors, nor by places, as one could other people.' It is too bad," Rowanna said quietly, "that more Quakers have not been legislators, Mr. Bright. Perhaps many of the evils in this world could have been avoided if all men were guided by the same principles which govern Quakers."

While Rowanna and his grandfather were speaking, Tobias slipped away. He had seen Judson approaching. Not yet having come to any decision regarding what he had seen, he had been scrupulously avoiding any contact with Judson.

"Tobias," Judson called after him, but Tobias feigned not to notice and lost himself in the crowd.

Judson stared after Tobias, perplexed. "Have you noticed," he asked Mr. Bright, "or am I imagining it? Is Tobias avoiding me for some reason?"

Joshua confessed that he too was puzzled by his grandson's actions these past few days. Tobias seemed unusually restless and disturbed. He slipped out of the house and was gone long periods during the day. Joshua had gone to check on Tobias for several nights, and the boy had not been in bed. When Joshua questioned him, he merely said the nights were too beautiful for just sleeping away, that he enjoyed the solitude, and the feeling the open sky gave him of the vastness of the universe. Probably no more than growing pains, Joshua conceded amiably.

"Perhaps," Judson said noncommittally. He frowned. He had not known that Tobias roamed abroad at night. How far did Tobias wander? What, if anything, did those keen young eyes see during his nocturnal meanderings?

"Excuse me," he said. He must find Tobias and speak with him. What had Tobias discovered? Certainly it was increasingly obvious that the boy was definitely shunning him, keeping his distance and his thoughts, whatever they were, to himself.

Small groups and large groups milled about the property; it was almost impossible for Judson to catch a glimpse of Tobias anywhere. Tobias, meanwhile, had allowed himself to be swallowed up by a group of Peru Blues, who were rehashing for the sixth or seventh time a skirmish, which one man insisted, with much laughter, upon calling the "Chipanue" war.

"You hear about the Peru Blues war, with the gallant Major Nimrod Makepeace Loofburrow leading his troops?" Jasper Lore asked Tobias. Jasper Lore was a big man, whose large head was covered with blond hair that sprouted on it like down. He had a receding forehead, a wide mouth with a heavy underlip and gray eyes that were small but keen. Laugh lines made deep indentations around his eyes and mouth. When he spoke, his voice was hearty, like the man himself.

"No, sir," Tobias said politely, glancing around. He could not see past Lore's bulk; the others in the group were pressing round again. Although the tale was wearing a little thin even for them, they were ready to hear Jasper retell it one more time. Judson, passing by, and overhearing Jasper begin his story, kept on going. He had heard all about the "Chipanue" war. Even if he were not intent upon finding Tobias, he would not have lingered to hear Jasper. The Peru Blues and their adventures held no interest for Judson.

"Well, now, sonny, let me tell you this here story right from the beginning," Jasper said, enjoying his new audience. "Word came to Peru that Indians were on the warpath up north. Yes sir, sonny," he repeated, delighted with Tobias' surprised glance, "that's the way we heard it. Indians were on the warpath up north."

159

The rumor had percolated through the town of Peru slowly at first, building up to a fine crescendo of fear mixed with anger. Rush Higgins, a commissioned officer in the militia, had sent a courier to Major Nimrod Makepeace Loofburrow. The Potawatomi, the courier had gasped, were rising in insurrection against the duly constituted authority of the United States government. The Major was to rally the Peru Blues and come to Colonel Higgins' aid at once.

The Major had leaped to action immediately. "Sound the drums. I want my company armed and ready for conflict," he had shouted. In a matter of moments the drummer was beating a steady tattoo — *rat-a-tat, rat-tat, rat-a-tat, rat-tat.* People began converging from all directions in answer to the insistent summons. The Major's voice could be heard snapping commands: *I want the men who are barefoot to separate from those wearing moccasins or shoes! The men carrying sticks and cornstalks are to drop out! I want men with rifles and guns only! Company, mount!*

The Major swung himself up on a splendid horse, some sixteen hands high, whose black coat, carefully groomed, gleamed almost iridescent in the sunlight. The horse with its good lines, long fine neck, well-sloped shoulders, and proud carriage to its head, lifted its good clean legs smartly as it pranced, eager to be off and running. The Major now discovered that there were more volunteers than horses! He pursed his lips; a walking militia would never arrive in time. Colonel Higgins had stressed haste.

The Major rode up and down before the men, who were now some forty in number. "We will impress horses as we march," he announced.

At the first farm just north of Peru, the Major spied a man plowing his field with two horses. He signaled his men to halt, and hailed the farmer to come close. Curious, the farmer, a man named Ratcliff Wilkinson, approached, mopping his forehead with the back of his hand, pushing his hat well back on his head.

"What you all dressed up for, Major?" he inquired genially, studying the Major's outfit. The Major, despite the need for haste, had nevertheless taken the time to don his uniform, a brilliant blue jacket decorated with ornate golden eagle buttons, his hat with its towering red plume, and gilded spurs.

"We need your horses, Ratcliff," the Major said brusquely.

"Is that a fact?" the other drawled. "Well, Major, I don't rightly know how to tell you, but so do I. Yes, sir, so do I. Nice seeing you boys," he told the men affably and started back across the field.

"Hold on there, Ratcliff," the Major roared. "I hope I don't have to point out your duty to you."

Wilkinson turned around. "My duty is to get this here field plowed. You want to play soldier, Major, you go right ahead. But don't come round here mouthing me about my duty because I'll tell you right out, talk like that just riles me." Once again Wilkinson began walking away.

"I'm pressing those horses into service," the Major snapped. "Boys, hop to it. Unhitch those horses."

161

"The first one that lays a hand on those horses will have his head busted," Wilkinson promised, clenching his fists. The muscles in his brawny arms tightened; he clamped his jaw forward pugnaciously; his eyes narrowed. He looked meaner than a fox in a hen house; the fight Wilkinson put up would surely go down in history.

Having impressed sufficient horses along their route, the Peru Blues galloped swiftly toward their goal. They passed the little village of Mexico, and had just come in sight of the Michigan Road, near where the new village of Rochester had recently been established, when they spotted another company of soldiers converging upon them. Both companies halted, and an exchange of information took place.

"The Potawatomi are on the warpath," Major Loofburrow reported to Captain G. M. Fitch, the commanding officer of the company from Logansport. "We are going to the rescue of Colonel Higgins."

"Major," the captain said patiently. "Indians in these parts have not been on the warpath since 1815. The *Colonel* is not in need of rescuing. It's the few Potawatomi who still remain who need our help."

"That's ridiculous," the Major replied hotly. "I received a message from the Colonel himself."

"Yes, sir. If you will call your men to attention, I will give them the true facts of the situation."

"We can get the true facts from Colonel Higgins," the Major insisted stubbornly. "There's no need to talk to my men. They'll follow me wherever I go."

"They have a right to the facts as I know them, Major." Captain Fitch insisted.

The men had gathered in closer to hear the dispute between their officers. Jasper Lore called out, "Let him talk, Major," and soon others took up his cry. Without waiting further permission, the Captain began to address the Peru Blues.

"Colonel Gallant is the United States paymaster who pays the Indians their annuities in this state," he said. "Colonel Higgins took the money away from Colonel Gallant, claiming that the Potawatomi owe him money for trade. The Potawatomi want their money back. And Colonel Gallant wants the money back so he can discharge his duty and pay the Indians the money that is due them. The Potawatomi are not threatening anyone: This is just an argument that is getting a little heated," he said, smiling. "Colonel Higgins, obviously, has called out the militia to help him keep the money. Colonel Gallant and the Potawatomi called on us to help them get the money back. And that is what we propose to do. I think we can persuade Colonel Higgins to do what's right, without full scale action," he added, looking obliquely at the Major's uniform, and the sword hanging handily in its scabbard by his side.

"I'd like to remind you that I outrank you," Major Loofburrow began stiffly.

Jasper Lore held a hurried consultation with the other members of the Peru Blues. "Uh, Major," he said, approaching the two officers, "me and the men

163

have been talking it over. We figure we'll go along with the Captain here. Where's this place, Captain?"

"The paying station, three miles north of Rochester. A place called Chipanue."

"Right. We'll go out on this Chipanue 'war' and see justice triumphs." Jasper winked at the Captain.

Momentarily, while Jasper was speaking, the Major had been rendered speechless. Now he roared, "You figure you'll go along with the Captain? I'm your commanding officer, and you will march where I tell you."

Jasper shook his head. "Now, Major," he said regretfully. "Me and the boys, we don't mind helping out where needful. But we sure enough aren't bill collectors. If that's what Colonel Higgins had in mind for us. And judging from what the Captain here says, that's about the size of it."

"That's right," a number of the men called out. "We'll just go along with the Captain."

"You can't relieve a commanding officer of his command in the field," the Major sputtered.

"Well, now, Major," Jasper said sunnily. "It looks like we just did, don't it?"

The Peru Blues had accompanied Captain Fitch and his man to Chipanue, had seen to it that Colonel Higgins had returned the boxes of money to the paymaster, had, in fact, helped load the boxes onto a wagon, and had taken it some three miles further to the north side of the Tippecanoe River. Both companies, the Peru Blues and the Logansport men, had guarded the boxes for three days until all the Potawatomi were paid.

"And we came back from our war," Jasper Lore finished his story with a flourish, "with not a single Jack of us lost! Except, in a manner of speaking, the Major!"

The men burst into a roar of laughter. "Get him," one man snickered. "Not a single Jack of us lost."

It was at this moment that the Major joined their group, dressed for the first time since Tobias had first seen him in civilian clothes. Without glancing at any of the men, he spoke directly to Tobias.

"Mr. Judson has been looking for you everywhere. He asks particularly that you meet him in an hour's time at the burning tree. Do you know which tree he means?"

Tobias nodded. Judson had shown Tobias the tree when they had first come. Judson had explained that back in 1836, this large hickory had caught fire. The fire had run up the tree about forty feet. There it had burned off, and then, slowly, constantly, had burned downward for nearly a year. It was known to one and all as the burning tree after that.

The Major then asked Tobias if he would walk a little way with him. Tobias joined him, and the two moved rapidly away from the group.

"I suppose," the Major said slowly, "that the men

165

have been telling you about the incident they like to call the Chipanue war?" The Major's voice was bitter.

"I'm sorry, sir," Tobias began, but Major Loofburrow cut him off abruptly.

"It's not important. I have received an offer from a post out West, where soldiers are still needed, and commanding officers command. I will be leaving Peru very shortly, but I did want to say goodbye to you and your grandfather, and hope that some day he will find his sister. If I do not manage to see him, will you tell him that for me?"

Once again Tobias started to apologize, and once again the Major waved the matter aside.

"Good luck to you, son," he said stiffly. As he left, he turned and called back over his shoulder, "Remember. In one hour. Under the burning tree."

CHAPTER

★ 11 ★

"Y<small>OU KNOW, DON'T YOU, T</small>OBIAS?" Judson asked quietly.

Tobias had come to the burning tree reluctantly, wanting desperately to be any place but at this rendezvous, but unable to disregard the summons. Now he looked at Judson with the anguish in his heart clearly written in his glance. He did not trust himself to speak, so he merely nodded.

"Have you been watching me at work in the cave?" Judson went on. Once again Tobias nodded.

After that first fateful night when he had seen Judson leading a horse beneath the stable, he had slipped out again and again when all were asleep in the household. Drawn irresistibly, he had moved like a shadow, blending his movements to the night sounds. He had gone at first because he wanted to convince himself that he had not seen Judson with a stolen horse. On succeeding nights, however, he had observed how cleverly Judson had disguised the horse. The light mane that had shimmered in the moonlight, the golden chestnut color, even the mare's diamond marking on the forehead — all were gone, vanished as if they had never been. Now another coal-black mare mingled with the other horses, ran with them across the pasture, came obediently to the stable when dusk fell, answered to the name "Midnight." Du Coeur's mare had been sold, Tobias had heard just that morning, with a group of other horses. Judson, after all, was a horse trader. People hereabouts were accustomed to seeing horses come and go.

"You haven't told anyone, have you, Tobias?" Judson's gaze was as clear and honest as it had ever been, but now it was puzzled as well.

"No," Tobias replied, so softly that Judson could barely hear him.

"Why not? I would have expected it . . . You know, Tobias, if you weren't a Quaker, I might have tried to bribe you somehow. Offer to send you to England, perhaps, to study under the great painters. Something that I know you might want. But the fact that you are a Quaker has defeated me." Judson laughed ruefully. "I insisted that you and your grandfather be my guests. How much better for me if your grandfather were not such a man of honor, and you not the true grandson of your grandfather! You know, Tobias, I have been expecting a hand to smite me almost every minute; I've even been expecting to see that zealot with the burning eyes — what was his name? Oh, yes, William Noble, the horse thief catcher — come riding in to hogtie me with his ropes." Judson put his head back and laughed heartily.

"How can thee take this so lightly?" Tobias blurted. "If thee is discovered, thee can go to prison."

"You're right, of course," Judson said at once, quite soberly. "I admit that the thought of prison chills me."

"Then why . . . ?"

"Then why steal horses?" Judson shrugged. "Would you believe me that I honestly don't know? I don't need the money; I'm a very rich man, you know, Tobias. And I don't need to find horses this way. I am, believe it or not, one of the best traders in this part of the country. The beauty of my operation is its simplicity. All my horses are sent on to Indianapolis and placed in livery stables there. From the livery stables, the horses are shipped out to all parts of the country. My reputation is impeccable. There isn't a livery stable in Indianapolis that isn't proud to have my horses. They know that the animals passing through my hands are bought and sold as safe investments. But that's not what you asked, is it, Tobias? You want to know why I steal, or how I got started stealing, anyway, I imagine." A reflective, withdrawn look suddenly made Judson seem quite different to Tobias. This was not the easy-going, pleasant, unruffled man Tobias was familiar with, but rather a moody, unhappy person who had never been permitted to emerge past the facade he had built over the years.

"It began almost as a joke," Judson went on so quietly he might almost be conversing with himself. "They made me president of the Peru Horse Thief Detective Association."

Judson could almost see the form that he had helped the new association draft. *We do hereby form ourselves into an association under the name of the Peru Horse Thief Detective Company for the purpose of detecting and arresting horse thieves, counterfeiters, incendiaries and all other fellows, and bringing them to Justice, to aid each other in the recovery of stolen property and for our mutual protection and indemnity against such thieves and fellows, as provided in said acts and amendments and in the manner particularly set out in the constitution and by-laws of this association and agree that this association shall exist for the period of ten years unless sooner dissolved by a vote of the majority of the members.*

"They were like boys in a little secret club," Judson continued. "Shall I quote the agreement each of us signed?" Without waiting for an answer from Tobias, Judson said, "*I do solemnly promise that I will keep sacred the secrets of the association and never speak the password above a whisper outside of a regular constituted order of the same and then only to a brother I know to be in good standing.* Et cetera, et cetera, et cetera.

"I wish you could have been at our meetings, Tobias. We changed the password every week. We had a special grip" — Judson grinned — "and we took up such important business at our meetings as passing

170

a resolution not to let gypsies — *gypsies*, Tobias! — camp near our rivers! Old Tom Sutton wanted a resolution to prohibit street fairs. Bill Remley wanted all gambling prohibited. And Squire Burck reported that one of his cows was missing!"

"Thee doesn't have to tell me," Tobias said miserably. "Thee doesn't owe me an explanation."

"But I do!" Judson seized Tobias by the arm earnestly. "It was a game at first, don't you see? I thought I would take a horse, disguise it, and then show them how clever I was in finding it. I never meant to keep it. But it was so easy! That first horse," a faraway look came into Judson's eyes, "I stole right under Asa Martin's nose." He laughed at Tobias' expression. "You're right, Tobias. I did it again, legally, in court. I enjoyed that! Our Miss Ashton is a very shrewd young woman. She knew that horse wasn't more than five years old. But that's the spice of it all, don't you see? Almost being caught. Almost. That's the key word. I'm a gambling man, Tobias. But not at cards, or dice, or horse races. A man can't control the turn of a card, the roll of the dice or a race. Unless he cheats. Stealing horses is different. There's excitement in it, and challenge, and danger." Judson's eyes danced. "And everything depends on the man himself, not on chance."

"Thee draws a fine distinction between cheating and stealing," Tobias said, bewildered.

"It's hard to explain." Judson frowned. "We aren't any of us perfect, Tobias. We're only human, my friend."

171

"Thee speaks as if to be human is to be weak. And that to call a weakness human is to make it acceptable," Tobias argued. "Or even excusable."

"How righteous you are," Judson sighed. "Now tell me, my good and righteous guest, why haven't you exposed me?"

"Thee speaks the word for me. My grandfather and I are guests in your home."

"Is that the only reason?"

"No. I *like* thee, Mr. Judson. I have liked thee from the first moment we met. I cannot be the instrument that brings thee down. Thee has nothing to fear from me," Tobias said, his voice thick with tears. Suddenly he could no longer go on with this conversation. He fled, leaving Judson beneath the burning tree, staring after him. He could not stand the thought of remaining on Judson's grounds and so fled across the creek, to seek sanctuary and peace on Little Bear Woman's land.

He ran until he was weary, then cast himself down beneath the quiet shade of a leafy oak. I will tell Grandfather that we must leave at once, he thought. The rally will be over tonight. Grandfather will have kept his promise. There is nothing to keep us here now.

Tobias had an intense longing to return home to Pennsylvania even though life there had been restricted. Never had he known such freedom as he had since coming to Indiana; never had he experienced so many exciting adventures. Nonetheless there came a time when one yearned for home and hearth again, and quiet times to rest one's soul. It was that time now for Tobias.

A voice spoke above him. Startled, Tobias sprang to his feet. The girl Akomia, Little Bear Woman's granddaughter, was standing there watching him. If she noticed his distress, she said nothing. She waited until he was calmer, then spoke.

"The horse races are beginning. I shall ride. Come and see," she commanded, then, without looking back to see if he was following, plunged through the woods. Tobias trailed in her wake; was ever a boy so beset by problems? He should not be attending a horse race. On the other hand, he had no desire to go back to the rally.

When Tobias caught up with Akomia, she smiled. A large crowd had already gathered, mostly Indians, but some people from Judson's rally had drifted across the creek and were now as eager to cheer the race as they had been minutes ago to applaud the speakers whooping it up for the Whigs.

"My grandmother had the first race track in Indiana," Akomia told Tobias. "She and my grandfather, Shepoconah, often raced along this track. The track went around four acres of corn and pumpkins." Akomia laughed. "There! Father is bringing out my pony. Wait here!" she commanded, running off to meet Jacques du Coeur, who greeted his daughter affectionately, smiling as she leaped lightly on the pony's back and trotted him off to the starting point.

Du Coeur joined Tobias. "I see that you and Akomia have met."

"I didn't know she was your daughter."

"Since I must travel often, Akomia lives with her grandmother Maconaquah, Little Bear Woman. Her mother, my wife Winona, died several years ago. A girl growing up needs to be with a woman. Maconaquah is a good woman."

"I find the Indian names pleasing to the ear," Tobias confessed. "Winona is a beautiful name."

"She was beautiful," du Coeur said abruptly, then, feeling that Tobias might think he was being rebuffed, added, "Winona means 'first born.' She was Maconaquah's first-born child. And also" — his face clouded — "the first to die."

While du Coeur was speaking, six Indians had been selected to judge the race. Two lined themselves up at the starting point, two trotted to the quarter stake, and two positioned themselves at the finish line.

"Clear the track! Clear the track!" a voice in the crowd called. It took several minutes before everyone milling about on the track left it clear for the riders. Someone fired a shot from a rifle. Akomia on her dappled-brown pony, a small animal which stood about twelve hands high, whipped triumphantly past a boy her own age astride a somewhat larger sorrel-colored roan. Akomia and the animal she rode seemed to flow together as a single entity. Momentarily Tobias experienced a feeling of unreality, as if the girl and pony were floating through the air in a dream sequence. Then Akomia laughed, and the sound of her voice brought Tobias back to reality.

"Some day I shall paint her, just as she looked when she passed me," Tobias said, and didn't know he had spoken aloud until du Coeur turned and regarded him speculatively.

"I won. I won," Akomia crowed, when she rejoined her father and Tobias. "I am better than all of them. I am like Maconaquah. When she was young, she too raced against all the braves. And Maconaquah was better than the best brave. Even better than Shepoconah."

While she was talking, another horse race had taken place. Now a squabble arose. A Miami had raced a Potawatomi. The Miami claimed victory; the Potawatomi stubbornly insisted the race was his. The judges conferred solemnly, and the decision was announced to the crowd.

"The race is even." The voice belonged to Little Bear Woman. "Winamac took the first quarter, Wawasee took the second quarter!"

"What is she saying?" Tobias asked. Before Akomia or du Coeur could reply, the announcement was made again, in English, for the benefit of the visitors from the Judson grounds.

Little Bear Woman pushed her way through the crowds and joined her son-in-law and granddaughter. She was a small woman, but she walked standing tall despite her age. She wore a blue calico dress. On the skirt dozens of narrow silk ribbons, intricately worked in a geometrical pattern, were layered one over the other creating one large elaborate design. She seemed to radiate light as she approached, for the sun danced

177

on her silver loop earrings and heavy silver necklace, and spun off into a myriad of reflecting beams. Her hair was sparse and gray, caught up behind her head and tied with worsted ferret, a smooth woolen cloth bound with the same silk ribbon decorating her skirt. Her face was heavily wrinkled and the skin dark and dry, much exposed to the elements, but still much lighter in color than either du Coeur's or Akomia's. There was a small scar on her left cheek, a memento she received when young at an Indian dance.

Akomia ran to greet her, and the old woman smiled at her briefly, then fixed her glance on Tobias, much as she had when Akomia had first brought him to her home, the night the starving wolves had attacked him. Unexpectedly, she now spoke to Tobias.

"What is she saying?" Tobias asked.

"She likes your hair," du Coeur said with a smile. "She says it is hair that flames in the sun."

Tobias smiled at her. "Since I have been here," Tobias told du Coeur, "I seem to forget to wear my hat. Grandfather scolds me, and he is right. I never used to forget to wear it in Pennsylvania."

The old woman spoke again.

It was Akomia who interpreted this time. "Grandmother asks what name you are called. She means other than Tobias."

Tobias shook his head. The old woman frowned. She had had many names. People changed as they grew. The names should change to fit their new personalities, their new deeds. Now she was called Maconaquah, Little Bear Woman. This was what Shepo-

178

conah had called her, and now that he was dead, this would remain her name until she too joined the Great Spirit. As a small child, she had been called "Kekeno-keshwah." Among the Delaware Indians, with whom she had lived a long time, Kekenokeshwah meant "cut finger." She had accidentally cut her finger on a knife while she was still very young.

Tobias stared at the old woman sharply. She had lived among the Delaware Indians? But he thought she was of the Miami tribe.

The old woman nodded patiently. Her husband was a Miami. But her father and mother had been Delawares. They had lived in the great rushing water place, where the water leaped from a palisade and hurtled downward in a perpendicular sheet of opacity, striking bottom so fiercely that the water sprang upward again, frothing, raging, as if to scale the forbidding cliff.

"Niagara Falls," du Coeur interpreted.

When she had married for the first time, her husband had also been a Delaware. It was Shepoconah who belonged to the Miami people, who had first called her Little Bear Woman. Her first husband's name for her was Wahkshingah, which means "moon lying crooked."

Du Coeur looked surprised. He had not known that Little Bear Woman had been married once before. She had never told anyone, he commented.

The old woman grinned at him good-naturedly. There were many things that Maconaquah had confided to no one, preferring to keep such matters to herself. It might astonish her son-in-law, she added mischievously, if she chose to tell him what she had always locked away in her heart.

Akomia had been translating rapidly for Tobias' sake. When she mentioned her grandmother's name — Wahkshingah, Moon Lying Crooked, Tobias said idly, "What is a moon lying crooked?"

"Have you never seen a moon lying crooked in the sky?" Akomia demanded. Tobias shook his head. Impatiently, Akomia sketched a picture in the dirt with the toe of her moccasin.

Staring down at the ground, Tobias felt as if a giant hand had reached out and crushed his chest. He found it difficult to breathe, even to swallow. His mouth, suddenly, was dry.

The old woman drew closer. She pointed at the moon lying crooked and smiled at Tobias. "Wahkshingah," she said. "Wahkshingah."

Tobias looked directly into the old woman's eyes. He had not noticed before, but they were curiously light, a chestnut brown that had faded somewhat over the years, but were still bright. A chill ran down his spine. Was it possible? Had the answer been here, all this while?

Du Coeur and Akomia had been watching Tobias, puzzled by his sudden silence and withdrawal.

"What is it?" Akomia asked. "What is happening?" She looked at Tobias and then at her grandmother. There seemed to be a communion of spirit between these two that excluded everyone else. "What is it?" she demanded again.

Du Coeur said, "You must be mistaken, Tobias. I see the direction your mind is going. Maconaquah is not white."

"She said there were many things that she kept locked in her heart," Tobias said slowly. He looked down at the rude sketch at his feet. Slowly he went closer to the old woman. "Wahkshingah?" he whispered.

Maconaquah's hands were held lightly folded one over the other. Gently Tobias reached forward. Grasping Maconaquah's hands, he turned them over slowly. There, in the palm of her right hand, faded, almost gone, but the familiar shape still apparent, was the mark Tobias had seen so often on his grandfather's palm.

"The crescent moon," Tobias said unbelievingly.

The long, long search had come to an end.

CHAPTER

★ 12 ★

$\mathcal{T}$OBIAS FELT SOMEWHAT DESOLATE, watching his grandfather and Maconaquah sitting side by side earnestly gazing into one another's eyes, together at long last yet divided by language and a lifetime of different experiences. In truth, it had begun as a desolate day.

Tobias had rushed back to the Judson household to tell his glad tidings and had been met at the door by a weeping Catherine and a distraught Mrs. Bladen. Joshua had appeared directly behind them, and it was he who had broken the news to Tobias that Judson had been arrested as a horse thief.

"Arrested?" Tobias repeated, sick at heart. Did Judson think that Tobias had betrayed him?

"I don't believe it. I'll never believe it," Catherine

flashed in her old imperious manner. "It was Asa Martin . . ."

"He overheard, he said, a conversation between you and Mr. Judson," Mrs. Bladen wailed, "at the burning tree."

"He couldn't have." Tobias denied vigorously. "There was no one around when Mr. Judson and I met."

"He was hiding nearby in the thicket," Joshua said bleakly. "How long has thee known?" he asked.

"Some little while. I saw Mr. Judson taking a stolen horse into his secret cave, under the stable . . ."

"A fairy tale," Catherine said contemptuously. "There is no secret cave under the stable. I have been out to that stable hundreds of times . . ." She faltered under Tobias' steady gaze and began to weep afresh. "I can't believe it. Mr. Judson has always been so kind, so gay, so understanding."

"And Asa Martin is such a mean man," Mrs. Bladen said wonderingly. "An ugly man, I always thought, inside and out. Yet he was the innocent victim, and Mr. Judson . . ." Her voice trailed off as she dabbed a handkerchief at her eyes.

"Where have they taken him?" Tobias asked.

"To jail." It was Catherine who replied. "Oh I can't bear to think of Mr. Judson in jail." She fled from the doorway back into the kitchen with Mrs. Bladen trailing in her wake.

Tobias followed Joshua into the house. "This is a sad day for all of us," Joshua said. It was only then that Tobias remembered his own news.

"I have made a drawing for thee, Grandfather," Tobias said, holding out a sheet with a pencil sketch on it.

"Thee has done what?" Joshua repeated with disbelief.

"Take it, Grandfather," Tobias urged. Joshua's eyes swept his grandson's face with outrage. "I think," Joshua said crisply, "that we have been overlong in Indiana. It is time for us to return to our home, Tobias, where thee can be among Friends again. I have been too lax . . ."

His voice trailed off. Tobias had thrust his drawing under his grandfather's nose. Joshua had no choice but to look down. It was a simple sketch, but powerfully drawn, of two hands, one in the other, palms up, the fingers bent and curling upward, obviously the hands of an aging woman. In the palm of the right hand there was visible, although not stressed, the outline of a crescent moon. Joshua studied the drawing at length, then lifted his eyes to Tobias and asked unsteadily, "What is the meaning of this drawing?"

"I have found Sarah," Tobias replied simply.

"Thee has found Sarah?" Joshua echoed incredulously. "Thee has found my little Sarah?"

"Not so little as all that, Grandfather," Tobias answered smiling. "She is not the little red-haired child thee remembers, Grandfather. She is old." Tobias broke off, a flush rising in his cheeks, as he remembered that Sarah and Joshua were twins.

"Do not let my age distress thee, Tobias." Joshua's eyes dimmed with tears. "Sarah. The search for Sarah

184

is over. How is it no one told us?" Joshua then demanded in a sudden change of mood, and refused to accept Tobias' explanation that Sarah had kept so important a fact to herself.

"Thee must remember that she has been an Indian all of her life, Grandfather," Tobias reminded Joshua gently. "She did not wish it known that she was white. Even her own children did not know it."

Joshua had rounded on Tobias angrily. "She is not an Indian." A vision of the small, merry-eyed, red-haired, mischievous Sarah popped into his mind. Sarah, who had teased Joshua and pouted because he was slower than she, but who had leaped like a lioness protecting her cub if anyone else dared criticize Joshua; Sarah, inventor of a hundred different games; Sarah, who mimicked others so well their mother was forced to laugh even as she chided the child for her unseemly conduct. "Sarah is as white as I am. She is my sister, my twin."

Tobias shook his head but said nothing.

He had led his grandfather across the creek to Maconaquah's house, where Maconaquah, Akomia and du Coeur awaited them. And now, while first Akomia and then du Coeur translated what brother had to say to sister, and sister to brother, Tobias sat and watched and was sad for both.

"Thee must come home with us, Sarah," Joshua said. "We are all the family thee has now."

"Joshua," Maconaquah said, the word strange on her lips. "No, I cannot, I have always lived with the Indians. They have used me most kindly. It is the

wish of the Great Spirit and my husband Shepoconah that I live and die with the Indians. On his death bed, Shepoconah charged me not to leave the Indians. Only Shepoconah knew that I was white, but the white blood had been washed from me long ago by my Indian father. I have a house and much land. I have a son-in-law and a granddaughter. My two sons and daughter are buried here. I have one hundred head of horses, cattle and hogs. I have clothes and calicoes. I have saddles and bridles. I am comfortable. Why should I go among strangers, and be like a fish out of water? No! I am glad to see my brother. But I will not leave this land."

"Then come and visit, Sarah," Joshua urged. "When thee sees how pleasant it is, thee will surely wish to stay. True, I do not have much; my farm is small and we live modestly. But thee will have a brother's love."

"Joshua." Once again the only English word on Maconaquah's lips sounded alien. She placed her hand over her brother's momentarily, then removed it quickly. "I cannot. I cannot. I am an old tree. I was a sapling when they took me away. It is all gone past. We cannot go back, Joshua. I would not be happy in the white world. And they would not be happy with me. I am glad to see my brother and his grandson. But I will never leave this place."

"Is this how the search is to end?" Joshua asked despairingly. "Have I spent a lifetime on this quest, only to have it end like this?"

"But thee was charged to do this," Tobias reminded

his grandfather, "and thee has kept the promise. It is not Maconaquah's fault . . ."

"Sarah," Joshua interjected automatically. His sister would never be anything but "Sarah" to him.

"Perhaps if Sarah were to tell us the things that befell her after she was stolen, thee will understand why she will not return with us, Grandfather."

Did Maconaquah remember the farm in Pennsylvania, her parents, her brother Isaac, her brother Nathan? Yes, Maconaquah recalled the broad-brimmed hat her father wore, her brother Isaac — her glance flashed to Tobias. When she had first seen Tobias, memories had surged back into her mind. She had thought much on the matter. Tobias seemed like someone from the long distant past, a dream she had once had perhaps.

Joshua nodded soberly. Tobias did indeed look very much like Isaac.

Maconaquah also remembered the farm near the Susquehannah. Wait, one other thing lingered: Joshua had limped.

Joshua's faced brightened. Yes, he had broken his leg, did Sarah remember? And that was why he had been left behind when the Indians had stolen Sarah. He limped, and the Indians thought he would hold them back.

They had traveled a long way, Maconaquah recalled, to a cave where the Indians had hidden some blankets. They had made a bed of leaves for the little girl. Next morning they had set off early; the sun had barely touched the sky with daylight. There were many days' journey ahead of them and the Indians wished to move as swiftly as possible.

"When we stopped at night, they made a bed of hemlock boughs for me," Maconaquah smiled reminiscently. "They made a great fire at their feet, to keep us warm, and to keep away the animals of the woods. They roasted meat by holding a stick with the meat on it over the fire. They drank at the brooks and springs and made me a little cup of birch bark to drink from. The water was sweet and delicious."

They were good to the little girl, who cried often at first. They gave her the best of the food they ate. When she grew tired, they carried her in their arms. It seemed to her that they were constantly on the move. They came to an Indian village, but they rested there but a few days.

Then early one morning, two of the Indians had come for Sarah. They had three horses, and placed her on the horse in the middle, riding single file, one leading, the other watching over the child with great care.

"I did not know there was so much land in the world," Maconaquah mused. The man who guided them was Ohúntamu, Horned Owl, an Indian chief who explained to the child that they were going north to his village where she would live from that time on. The village was large and teeming with people and many dogs. When they arrived, the dogs circled around them, barking wildly, and the women had flocked to their sides, reaching out to touch Sarah's hair, while the small children stared at her with sur-

prise in their dark eyes. At first she had stayed in
Horned Owl's wigwam, a dwelling that she had sur-
veyed doubtfully, never having seen such a structure
before. It was an oval-shaped hut constructed with
poles that had been overlaid with bent branches covered with bark and animal skins.

Sarah soon grew accustomed to the sound of the
great falls and even learned to take it for granted although in the beginning the thunderous roar pervaded
her days. Little by little she discovered that the Indian
words began to take on meaning for her. She was
adaptable and before long was adept in the simple
tasks they assigned to her.

One morning Horned Owl surprised her. He led her
gently by the hand down the hill from their wigwam
to the river. She must wash in the river, Horned Owl
said, wash away in the clear waters all traces of her
white blood, for from this day forward she would be
truly one of the Indian people. This day Horned Owl
would bring her to her new father and mother. When
she came out of the water, Horned Owl rearranged her
beautiful red hair, after the fashion of the Indian
women. And he gave her a deerskin dress, which one
of the women had painstakingly decorated with dyed
porcupine quills and beads, and handed her a pair of
moccasins, which were also beautifully adorned. He
placed wampum beads tenderly about her neck and
finally, with great care, painted her face.

"Come, Ntaan," Horned Owl had said, holding out
his hand. Ntaan, Maconaquah explained in an

aside to Joshua and the others, was the Delaware word for "my daughter." Horned Owl had not adopted her, but he had called her Ntaan from the moment they had arrived in the Indian village fronting the Niagara River. Ntaan had taken Ohúntamu's hand obediently, walking with him along the river's edge to a wigwam where an old man and woman lived.

"I thought they were old, then," Maconaquah said, laughing. "Now that I myself am old, I can understand that they were not so old as they looked to me."

Du Coeur smiled at his mother-in-law, and continued translating Maconaquah's story.

"They had had children, but all had died, some in the wars, others when they were still quite small. They were most unwilling to adopt me at first. They did not want a daughter with red hair. Red hair was not natural, they argued.

They would rather have an Indian child, they told Ohúntamu, although they knew that white children were often kidnapped to replace Indian children who had died. But Horned Owl had been most persuasive. Ntaan was sad to leave Horned Owl's wigwam, for she had lived there for many months, and she had grown to love him. But Ohúntamu did not have a wife, and his own daughter was too young to be a mother to Ntaan.

"It was now the fall of the year, for the chestnuts had come," Maconaquah said, her eyes seemingly turned inward as she went back into the past she had never discussed with her children or her son-in-law.

191

Du Coeur and Akomia were listening raptly, for her reminiscences were as fresh to them as they were to Joshua and Tobias.

Ntaan, whose name had once again been changed, this time to Ahpu, meaning "she stays," remained with her new parents in the village for the balance of the winter. There was much excitement, for the British and the Americans eyed each other like snarling dogs. The British armed the Indians with many rifles and much ammunition.

"The British and the Americans had a war," Maconaquah recalled, "and when the Americans came near the fort where we lived, they drove us away. But the Indians took many scalps."

Joshua's lips parted; he seemed about to comment, but Tobias laid a restraining hand on his arm. The child who had the white blood washed away in the cleansing waters of the river, the girl growing up in a culture that was woven into the warp and woof of her days, why would she not rejoice in the triumph of those who were now her people?

As Ahpu, she recalled, she had gone with her parents to live near Detroit, where they stayed for three years, and then moved on again with one other Delaware family to a new home on the Eel River, not far from Fort Wayne.

"The Delawares were good. They treated me kindly," Maconaquah insisted, but then her eyes grew dark, for she was now approaching a time that had left scars on her spirit. "But there was one who spoke falsely, one who called himself a warrior. It was he who gave me a new name — Moon Lying Crooked. For many years he was my husband, yet we had no children. For this he beat me, taunting me, saying that I was barren, shouting that a tree that had no fruit should not be permitted to blossom. Yet he would not let me go, for it pleased him that I was white and that my hair flamed in the sun. No other brave had such a wife. No other woman among the Delawares had such a husband," she commented bitterly. "He came to me one day insisting that I go west with him across the great Mississippi, but I would not go. I would not leave my people. He beat me and left me as one dead. But I would not die for such a one as he. Never!"

The Delawares and the Miami were living together as one people. Maconaquah went on after a pause, resolutely putting from her mind all thought of the husband, who remained nameless, who had fled west of the Mississippi and had never been heard from again. And then she had met Shepoconah. When she spoke his name, Maconaquah's voice softened, her eyes grew misty.

"I know this story," Akomia exclaimed. "How Maconaquah and Shepoconah first met."

"And I, too," du Coeur said with a grin. "I cannot tell you how many times that tale has been repeated to us."

"It was most romantic," Akomia insisted. She turned eagerly to Joshua and Tobias and began to

193

relate the incident as if she had been an eye witness.

There had been a skirmish between the soldiers and the Indians. When it was over, many wounded lay on the field of battle. Maconaquah had gone among them to succor those she could. Heartsick at the sight of the dying, she had fled to a nearby glade to allow its peacefulness to refresh her soul. Leaning her head against a tree, she closed her eyes to savor the stillness of the woods. She had heard a sound then, a muffled cry instantly stifled. Stiffening, she glanced quickly around, but she was alone except for birds that darted overhead and a squirrel who sat some distance away at the foot of a birch regarding her with a steady, watchful bright-eyed stare, its forepaws frozen in mid-air. The cry came again. The squirrel leaped across the ground and vanished up a tree. Maconaquah stood, head cocked, trying to locate the direction of the sound.

When it came again, she pinpointed it to a hollow log that lay just across the glade. Maconaquah approached it warily, dropped to her knees and peered inside. A young man lay there, his fist to his mouth, trying to suppress the moans which rose to his lips.

"How can I help you?" Maconaquah cried.

"Go away," he replied with difficulty. "I wish no one here to see me die."

"You must come out and let me tend to your wounds," Maconaquah insisted. The brave closed his eyes. "Let me be," he murmured. "Let me be." His voice faded; his eyes remained shut.

"You will not die," Maconaquah snapped. "I forbid

it." The young man lapsed into unconsciousness, but evidently had heard her words, for the ghost of a smile hovered about his lips.

Maconaquah, pulling, straining, exerting every muscle, at last freed him from the hollow log where he had crawled to greet death. She stretched him out on the ground, studied his injuries, tended to him as best she could, then ran fleetly to get help.

From that moment on, it had been a contest of wills, the young man resigned to death, the young woman battling for his life. He proved no match for her. In time his wounds healed, but his heart was troubled. He had never expected to take a white woman as his bride, for he had no great love for the whites, he declared. Maconaquah said passionately that she was not white, that she had been cleansed of white blood many years ago, that she was as much Delaware as Shepoconah. Shepoconah smiled and said his new bride's heart flamed as fiery as her hair; it was strong medicine, but he was a strong man. He called her his "little bear woman," Maconaquah, and that was how she got her name. She would never be called anything else ever again.

"Maconaquah," Joshua said, testing it, then shook his head. "Thee has always been Sarah to me. It is not easy to change the habits of a lifetime."

No, Maconaquah agreed at once, and that was why she would remain here. She could not give up a lifetime of Indian living to take up her place among white people again. Surely Joshua could understand. Here she and Shepoconah had had their children; here she had buried her husband and sons and a daughter. They had come to Indiana, had lived in Deaf Man's Village — so-called because Shepoconah had become deaf, then had moved here and claimed the land on which this house had been built, and here she would stay until the Great Spirit called.

★ Epilogue ★

1845

October 5, 1845

M<small>Y VERY DEAR</small> T<small>OBIAS:</small>

It seems so long a time since we had a letter from you! Of course we continue to get the news of your doings through Jacques du Coeur, who very graciously keeps us informed, knowing of our great and continued interest in you. And your grandfather, too, is kind enough to share his letters.

Your grandfather, I think, is reconciled by now to your living in London as a student of the Royal Academy of Art. The miracle of miracles is that he was persuaded to let you attend at all!

Rowanna bit thoughtfully at the end of her quill pen. She remembered that scene, when Jacques du

Coeur had approached Joshua Bright on Tobias' behalf.

"You must allow me to do this," du Coeur had insisted. "I am a rich man. Indeed, rumor has it," du Coeur said, his eyes twinkling, "that I have so much money that I bury it in pots here and there along the river, or under the house, or even in the cemetery. So you see, my friend, your grandson will be well cared for."

"The boy's place is here with me," Joshua was equally insistent. Since his sister Sarah had refused to leave her home in Indiana to accompany him to Pennsylvania, Joshua had decided to remain near her. He had approached du Coeur rather diffidently; he knew, Joshua said, that Miss Ashton was being most helpful in du Coeur's attempts to establish a school for Indian children. But the young men needed help, too, and he, Joshua, would like to teach them new ways of farming. Their present methods were slow and hard. It was time they learned to use a plow, and certainly they would find the use of the wooden horse rake invaluable. ("Does thee know that with this new invention one man with one horse can do as much work as eight braves using hand rakes?" Joshua had persisted.)

"You will never make a farmer of Tobias," du Coeur had told Joshua bluntly. "I am delighted to accept your offer of help. I will be glad to purchase whatever equipment you think my people will need for modern farming. But the boy's talents lie elsewhere. My friend," du Coeur continued persuasively, "many men may learn to farm, but few have the special gifts Tobias has. They are God-given. Why do you fight this?"

"It is forbidden," Joshua reiterated.

Rowanna caught Joshua's hand in her own. "Oh, Mr. Bright, I beg you. Don't condemn Tobias to a lifetime of yearning for a will-o'-the-wisp, a tantalizing dream. Let him go. If he is a poor artist, he will find it out soon enough. He will be a better farmer for it, I promise you. But if he is as gifted as we think he is, he will truly find himself. He can become a bitter, frustrated man, or one who fulfills his destiny. Mr. Bright" — Rowanna's eyes filled with tears — "so few of us contribute anything. Our days pass like shadows, and when we die, we leave no sign that we were here. Don't deny Tobias his right to mark his passage on Earth."

"If you don't," du Coeur warned, "you may find that Tobias will abandon the religion that puts these fetters on his spirit. Better to have a boy who strays a small way from the path than one who forsakes the path completely."

"I am an old man," Joshua said sadly, "and confused. I came to find a sister, and now it seems I must lose a grandson."

"Never," Rowanna cried triumphantly, for it was obvious to her that Joshua was capitulating. She could see Tobias' future glowing golden with promise. "By setting him free, you have only made more certain of his love."

Joshua had placed a handkerchief to his nose and

blown it noisily. "Why are women so dramatic and emotional over the simplest matters?" he had demanded testily.

Remembering how Joshua had surreptitiously fingered away a few tears of his own, Rowanna now smiled down at her letter, and then looked up again at a slight sound. She put her pen down hastily and hastened to a cradle in the corner of the room. "Well, Sarah?" she said softly. "Are you awake?" The infant stared upward with eyes still awash with sleep, yawned, and waved small clenched fists in the air. "And hungry?" Rowanna asked tenderly. For now, the letter must be put aside.

How much had happened in the five years since Tobias had left for England, Rowanna reflected.

Maconaquah's illness had come on suddenly, and she had failed under everyone's eyes. Joshua had been desolate.

"Would thee leave me yet again, Sarah?" he wept. He had steadfastly refused to call her Maconaquah. She had laid a weak hand over his.

"Thee will find me, Joshua," she whispered, the words coming clear to her mind as if the intervening years had become compressed.

"Sarah!" Joshua said, but she was gone.

Maconaquah was buried beside her husband, as she had wished. Above her grave, du Coeur placed a pole from which there fluttered in the breeze the white flag which would enable the Great Spirit to know where to find her. Joshua did not object, but long after the others had departed from the grave site, he lingered silently with head bowed. Rowanna had gone back to him. Touching him gently, she had led the saddened brother away.

Rowanna now returned to her letter, leaving Sarah to play contentedly while she wrote.

As you know, when I married Pierre Le Cateau three years ago, the Indian school was thriving. I continued teaching there until last year, when our own little Sarah was born.

Rowanna looked over at her daughter, who, catching her mother's eye, gurgled up at her. How pleased Joshua had been when Rowanna had told him the infant would be christened Sarah Bright Le Cateau. Long ago a small Sarah Bright had vanished and her name with her. Now a new Sarah Bright would grow to young womanhood and perhaps, the new mother speculated, watching little Sarah proudly, bring honor again to the name.

Akomia, Rowanna brought her wandering thoughts back to the letter, *took over the school when I left, and is doing a splendid job with the youngsters. She has grown into a remarkably pretty young lady and is much sought after, but she is completely dedicated to her work.*

You will already have heard from your grandfather about Mr. Judson's escape from prison. He was a model prisoner, I am told, and was trusted completely. He was always a man who gave one the impression of candor and reliability. There are many rumors, of course, regarding his present whereabouts; I myself am inclined to believe those people who say he has un-

doubtedly fled westward and is already busy establishing a new identity.

You will be saddened, I think, to learn that Major Loofburrow (surely you remember the Major?) was killed in a skirmish between army troops and Apache raiders in Arizona. Their leader, I believe, is an Apache Indian chief whose name is Cochise. When I see how peacefully we live with our Indian brothers here in Indiana, it is hard for me to visualize the violence that still flows between the white man and the red man farther west.

I know that many here were inclined to regard the Major as somewhat of a pompous fool, but I found him always gentle and considerate, and I do mourn his passing.

The only other bit of news I have to impart, and it is not yet certain so I trust you will not speak of it yet . . . Pierre has been approached as a possible candidate to stand for election as a United States Senator! He has served the people well in the State Legislature, and now, if he is chosen, will serve them equally well in our nation's capital.

This letter threatens to become a mighty tome! Write to us when you can spare the time, Tobias. We expect to hear great news from you regarding your forthcoming exhibit in London.

Your very good friend,
Rowanna Ashton Le Cateau

Rowanna folded and enclosed her letter in an envelope. As she addressed it, she found herself wondering again what strange loom of destiny had woven the lives of all the people she had mentioned and then refashioned the design. What did life hold in store in the years to come? Who could say?

STETTLER MUNICIPAL LIBRARY

Bibliography

Alvord's History of Noble County, Indiana. Logansport, Indiana: B. F. Bowen, 1902.

Banta, David D. *Historical Sketch of Johnson County.* Chicago, Illinois: J. H. Beers Co., 1881.

Clarkson, Thomas. *A View of the Moral Education, Discipline, Peculiar Customs, Religious Principles, Political and Civil Economy, and Character of the Society of Friends.* ("A Portrait of Quakerism.") Indianapolis, Indiana: Merrill and Field, 1870.

Cockrum, William M. *Pioneer History of Indiana.* Oakland City, Indiana: Press of the Oakland City Journal, 1907.

Cox, Sandford C. *Recollections of the Early Settlement of the Wabash Valley.* Lafayette, Indiana: Courier Steam Book and Job Printing House, 1860. Reproduced by Hossier Heritage Press, Indianapolis, Indiana.

Crawfordsville (Indiana) *Journal.* May 30, 1908, June 1, 1908; June 5, 1908.

The Early Settlement of the Miami Country. (Letters to Oliver B. Torbet from Dr. Ezra Ferris.) Lawrenceburg, Indiana: Independent Press, 1850–51.

Feder, Norman. *American Indian Art.* New York: Harry N. Abrams, 1969.

Greenbie, Sydney. *Frontiers and the Fur Trade.* New York: John Day Co., 1929.

Harden, Samuel, compiler. *The Pioneer.* Greenfield, Indiana: William Mitchell Printing Co., 1895.

History of Pike and Dubois Counties. Chicago, Illinois: Goodspeed Bros. Co., 1885.

Indiana History Bulletin. Indianapolis, Indiana: Indiana Historical Bureau, March 1972.

Montgomery, M. W. *History of Jay County.* Chicago, Illinois: Church, Goodman and Cushing, 1864.

Papers of Thomas and Sarah Pears. (Letters to Benjamin Bakewell, 1825.) Indianapolis, Indiana: Indiana Historical Society Publications, 1933.

Stephens, John H. *History of Miami Country.* Peru, Indiana: John H. Stephens Publishing House, 1896.

Turpie, David. *Sketches of My Own Times.* Indianapolis, Indiana: Bobbs-Merrill Co., 1903.

Wendell, E., Josephine Lamb, and Lawrence W. Schultz, compilers. *More Indian Lore.* Winona Lake, Indiana: Published by the authors, printed by Light and Life Press, 1968.

Whitmore, William H. *The Elements of Heraldry.* Rutland, Vermont: Charles E. Tuttle Co., 1968.

Winger, Otho. *The Frances Slocum Trail.* Published by the author, printed in North Manchester, Indiana, 1933.

Winter, George. *Journal of a Visit to Deaf Man's Village,* 1839. Tippecanoe County Historical Museum. Reproduced in *The Journals and Indian Paintings of George Winter, 1837–39.* Indianapolis, Indiana: Indianapolis Historical Society, 1948.

DoB. $\mathcal{J}$ 13136

Stettler Municipal Library
Stettler, Alberta

RULES

1. Books may be kept two weeks in town and three weeks out of town.

2. A fine of five cents a week will be charged on each book which is not returned according to the above rule. No book will be issued to any person incurring such a fine until it has been paid.

3. All injuries to books, beyond reasonable wear, and all losses shall be made good to the satisfaction of the **Librarian**.

4. Each borrower is held responsible for all books drawn on his card and for all fines accruing on the same.

STETTLER MUNICIPAL LIBRARY

$\mathcal{J}$ 13136